Sacred And Profane Love

Arnold Bennett

I

For years I had been preoccupied with thoughts of love—and by love I mean a noble and sensuous passion, absorbing the energies of the soul, fulfilling destiny, and reducing all that has gone before it to the level of a mere prelude. And that afternoon in autumn, the eve of my twenty-first birthday, I was more deeply than ever immersed in amorous dreams.

I, in my modern costume, sat down between two pairs of candles to the piano in the decaying drawing-room, which like a spinster strove to conceal its age. A generous fire flamed in the wide grate behind me: warmth has always been to me the first necessary of life. I turned round on the revolving stool and faced the fire, and felt it on my cheeks, and I asked myself: 'Why am I affected like this? Why am I what I am?' For even before beginning to play the Fantasia of Chopin, I was moved, and the tears had come into my eyes, and the shudder to my spine. I gazed at the room inquiringly, and of course I found no answer. It was one of those rooms whose spacious and consistent ugliness grows old into a sort of beauty, formidable and repellent, but impressive; an early Victorian room, large and stately and symmetrical, full—but not too full—of twisted and tortured mahogany, green rep, lustres, valances, fringes, gilt tassels. The green and gold drapery of the two high windows, and here and there a fine curve in a piece of furniture, recalled the Empire period and the deserted Napoleonic palaces of France. The expanse of yellow and green carpet had been married to the floor by two generations of decorous feet, and the meaning of its tints was long since explained away. Never have I seen a carpet with less individuality of its own than that carpet; it was so sweetly faded, amiable, and flat, that its sole mission in the world seemed to be to make things smooth for the chairs. The wall-paper looked like pale green silk, and the candles were reflected in it as they were reflected in the crystals of the chandelier. The grand piano, a Collard and Collard, made a vast mass of walnut in the chamber, incongruous, perhaps, but still there was something in its mild and indecisive tone that responded to the furniture. It, too, spoke of Evangelicalism, the Christian Year, and a dignified reserved confidence in Christ's blood. It, too, defied the assault of time and the invasion of ideas. It, too, protested against Chopin and romance, and demanded Thalberg's variations on 'Home, Sweet Home.'

My great-grandfather, the famous potter—second in renown only to Wedgwood—had built that Georgian house, and my grandfather had furnished it; and my parents, long since dead, had placidly accepted it and the ideal that it stood for; and it had devolved upon my Aunt Constance, and ultimately it would devolve on me, the scarlet woman in a dress of virginal white, the inexplicable offspring of two changeless and blameless families, the secret revolutionary, the living lie! How had I come there?

I went to the window, and, pulling the curtain aside, looked vaguely out into the damp, black garden, from which the last light was fading. The red, rectangular house stood in the midst of the garden, and the garden was surrounded by four brick walls, which preserved it from four streets where dwelt artisans of the upper class. The occasional rattling of a cart was all we caught of the peaceable rumour of the town; but on clear nights the furnaces of Cauldon Bar Ironworks lit the valley for us, and we were reminded that our refined and inviolate calm was hemmed in by rude activities. On the east border of the garden was a row of poplars, and from the window I could see the naked branches of the endmost. A gas-lamp suddenly blazed behind it in Acre Lane, and I descried a bird in the tree. And as the tree waved its plume in the night-wind, and the bird swayed on the moving twig, and the gas-lamp burned meekly and patiently beyond, I seemed to catch in these simple things a glimpse of the secret meaning of human existence, such as one gets sometimes, startlingly, in a mood of idle receptiveness. And it was so sad and so beautiful, so full of an ecstatic melancholy, that I dropped the curtain. And my thought ranged lovingly over our household—prim, regular, and perfect: my old aunt embroidering in the breakfast-room, and Rebecca and Lucy ironing in the impeachable kitchen, and not one of them with the least suspicion that Adam had not really waked up one morning minus a rib. I wandered in fancy all over the house—the attics, my aunt's bedroom so miraculously neat, and mine so unkempt, and the dark places in the corridors where clocks ticked.

I had the sense of the curious compact organism of which my aunt was the head, and into which my soul had strayed by some caprice of fate. What I felt was that the organism was suspended in a sort of enchantment, lifelessly alive, unconsciously expectant of the magic touch which would break the spell, and I wondered how long I must wait before I began to live. I know now that I was happy in those serene preliminary years, but nevertheless I had the illusion of spiritual woe. I sighed grievously as I went back to the piano, and opened the volume of Mikuli's Chopin.

Just as I was beginning to play, Rebecca came into the room. She was a maid of forty years, and stout; absolutely certain of a few things, and quite satisfied in her ignorance of all else; an important person in our house, and therefore an important person in the created universe, of which our house was for her the centre. She wore the white cap with distinction, and when an apron was suspended round her immense waist it ceased to be an apron, and became a symbol, like the apron of a Freemason.

'Well, Rebecca?' I said, without turning my head.

I guessed urgency, otherwise Rebecca would have delegated Lucy.

'If you please, Miss Carlotta, your aunt is not feeling well, and she will not be able to go to the concert to-night.'

'Not be able to go to the concert!' I repeated mechanically.

'No, miss.'

'I will come downstairs.'

'If I were you, I shouldn't, miss. She's dozing a bit just now.'

'Very well.'

I went on playing. But Chopin, who was the chief factor in my emotional life; who had taught me nearly all I knew of grace, wit, and tenderness; who had discovered for me the beauty that lay in everything, in sensuous exaltation as well as in asceticism, in grief as well as in joy; who had shown me that each moment of life, no matter what its import, should be lived intensely and fully; who had carried me with him to the dizziest heights of which passion is capable; whose music I spiritually comprehended to a degree which I felt to be extraordinary—Chopin had almost no significance for me as I played then the most glorious of his compositions. His message was only a blurred sound in my ears. And gradually I perceived, as the soldier gradually perceives who has been hit by a bullet, that I was wounded.

The shock was of such severity that at first I had scarcely noticed it. What? My aunt not going to the concert? That meant that I could not go. But it was impossible that I should not go. I could not conceive my absence from the concert—the concert which I had been anticipating and preparing for during many weeks. We went out but little, Aunt Constance and I. An oratorio, an amateur operatic performance, a ballad concert in the Bursley Town Hall—no more than that; never the Hanbridge Theatre. And now Diaz was coming down to give a pianoforte recital in the Jubilee Hall at Hanbridge; Diaz, the darling of European capitals; Diaz, whose name in seven years had grown legendary; Diaz, the Liszt and the Rubenstein of my generation, and the greatest interpreter of Chopin since Chopin died—Diaz! Diaz! No such concert had ever been announced in the Five Towns, and I was to miss it! Our tickets had been taken, and they were not to be used! Unthinkable! A photograph of Diaz stood in a silver frame on the piano; I gazed at it fervently. I said: 'I will hear you play the Fantasia this night, if I am cut in pieces for it to-morrow!' Diaz represented for me, then, all that I desired of men. All my dreams of love and freedom crystallized suddenly into Diaz.

SACRED AND PROFANE LOVE

I ran downstairs to the breakfast-room.

'You aren't going to the concert, auntie?' I almost sobbed.

She sat in her rocking-chair, and the gray woollen shawl thrown round her shoulders mingled with her gray hair. Her long, handsome face was a little pale, and her dark eyes darker than usual.

'I don't feel well enough,' she replied calmly.

She had not observed the tremor in my voice.

'But what's the matter?' I insisted.

'Nothing in particular, my dear. I do not feel equal to the exertion.'

'But, auntie—then I can't go, either.'

'I'm very sorry, dear,' she said. 'We will go to the next concert.'

'Diaz will never come again!' I exclaimed passionately. 'And the tickets will be wasted.'

'My dear,' my Aunt Constance repeated, 'I am not equal to it. And you cannot go alone.'

I was utterly selfish in that moment. I cared nothing whatever for my aunt's indisposition. Indeed, I secretly accused her of maliciously choosing that night of all nights for her mysterious fatigue.

'But, auntie,' I said, controlling myself, 'I must go, really. I shall send Lucy over with a note to Ethel Ryley to ask her to go with me.'

'Do,' said my aunt, after a considerable pause, 'if you are bent on going.'

I have often thought since that during that pause, while we faced each other, my aunt had for the first time fully realized how little she knew of me; she must surely have detected in my glance a strangeness, a contemptuous indifference, an implacable obstinacy, which she had never seen in it before. And, indeed, these things were in my glance. Yet I loved my aunt with a deep affection. I had only one grievance against her. Although excessively proud, she would always, in conversation with men, admit her mental and imaginative inferiority, and that of her sex. She would admit, without being asked, that being a woman she could not see far, that her feminine brain could not carry an argument to the end, and that her feminine purpose was too infirm for any great enterprise. She seemed to find a morbid pleasure in such confessions. As regards herself, they were accurate enough; the dear creature was a singularly good judge of her own character. What I objected to was her assumption, so calm and gratuitous, that her individuality, with all its confessed limitations, was, of course, superior—stronger, wiser, subtler than mine. She never allowed me to argue with her; or if she did, she treated my remarks with a high, amused tolerance. 'Wait till you grow older,' she would observe, magnificently ignorant of the fact that my soul was already far older than hers. This attitude naturally made me secretive in all affairs of the mind, and most affairs of the heart.

We took in the county paper, the *Staffordshire Recorder,* and the *Rock* and the *Quiver*. With the help of these organs of thought, which I detested and despised, I was supposed to be able to keep discreetly and sufficiently abreast of the times. But I had other aids. I went to the Girls' High School at Oldcastle till I was nearly eighteen. One of the mistresses there used to read continually a red book covered with brown paper. I knew it to be a red book because the paper was gone at the corners. I admired the woman immensely, and her extraordinary interest in the book—she would pick it up at every spare moment—excited in me an ardent curiosity. One day I got a chance to open it, and I read on the title-page, *Introduction to the Study of Sociology*, by Herbert Spencer. Turning the pages, I encountered some remarks on Napoleon that astonished and charmed me. I said: 'Why are not our school histories like this?' The owner of the book caught me. I asked her to lend it to me, but she would not, nor would she give me any reason for declining. Soon afterwards I left school. I persuaded my aunt to let me join the Free Library at the Wedgwood Institution. But the book was not in the catalogue. (How often, in exchanging volumes, did I not gaze into the reading-room, where men read the daily papers and the magazines, without daring to enter!) At length I audaciously decided to buy the book. I ordered it, not at our regular stationer's in Oldcastle Street, but at a little shop of the same kind in Trafalgar Road. In three days it arrived. I called for it, and took it home secretly in a cardboard envelope-box. I went to bed early, and I began to read. I read all night, thirteen hours. O book with the misleading title—for you have nothing to do with sociology, and you ought to have been called *How to Think Honestly*—my face flushed again and again as I perused your ugly yellowish pages! Again and again I exclaimed: 'But this is marvellous!' I had not guessed that anything so honest, and so courageous, and so simple, and so convincing had ever been written. I am capable now of suspecting that Spencer was not a supreme genius; but he taught me intellectual courage; he taught me that nothing is sacred that will not bear inspection; and I adore his memory. The next morning after breakfast I fell asleep in a chair. 'My dear!' protested Aunt Constance. 'Ah,' I thought, 'if you knew, Aunt Constance, if you had the least suspicion, of the ideas that are surging and shining in my head, you would go mad—go simply mad!' I did not care much for deception, but I positively hated clumsy concealment, and the red book was in the house; at any moment it might be seized. On a shelf of books in my bedroom was a novel called *The Old Helmet*, probably the silliest novel in the world. I tore the pages from the binding and burnt them; I tore the binding from Spencer and burnt it; and I put my treasure in the covers of *The Old Helmet*. Once Rebecca, a person privileged, took the thing away to read; but she soon brought it back. She told me she had always understood that *The Old Helmet* was more, interesting than that.

Later, I discovered *The Origin of Species* in the Free Library. It finished the work of corruption. Spencer had shown me how to think; Darwin told me what to think. The whole of my upbringing went for naught thenceforward. I lived a double life. I said nothing to my aunt of the miracle wrought within me, and she suspected nothing. Strange and uncanny, is it not, that such miracles can escape the observation of a loving heart? I loved her as much as ever, perhaps more than ever. Thank Heaven that love can laugh at reason!

So much for my intellectual inner life. My emotional inner life is less easy to indicate. I became a woman at fifteen—years, interminable years, before I left school. I guessed even then, vaguely, that my nature was extremely emotional and passionate. And I had nothing literary on which to feed my dreams, save a few novels which I despised, and the Bible and the plays and poems of Shakespeare. It is wonderful, though, what good I managed to find in those two use-worn volumes. I knew most of the Song of Solomon by heart, and many of the sonnets; and I will not mince the fact that my favourite play was *Measure for Measure*. I was an innocent virgin, in the restricted sense in which most girls of my class and age are innocent, but I obtained from these works many a lofty pang of thrilling pleasure. They illustrated Chopin for me, giving precision and particularity to his messages. And I was ashamed of myself. Yes; at the bottom of my heart I was ashamed of myself because my sensuous being responded to the call of these masterpieces. In my ignorance I thought I was lapsing from a sane and proper ideal. And then—the second miracle in my career, which has been full of miracles—I came across a casual reference, in the *Staffordshire Recorder*, of all places, to the *Mademoiselle de Maupin* of Théophile Gautier. Something in the reference, I no longer remember what, caused me to guess that the book was a revelation of matters hidden from me. I bought it. With the assistance of a dictionary, I read it, nightly, in about a week. Except *Picciola*, it was the first French novel I had ever read. It held me throughout; it revealed something on nearly every page. But the climax dazzled and blinded me. It was exquisite, so high and pure, so startling, so bold, that it made me ill. When I recovered I had fast in my heart's keeping the new truth that in the body, and the instincts of the body, there should be no shame, but rather a frank, joyous pride. From that moment I ceased to be ashamed of anything that I honestly liked. But I dared not keep the book. The knowledge of its contents would have killed my aunt. I read it again; I read the last pages several times, and then I burnt it and breathed freely.

Such was I, as I forced my will on my aunt in the affair of the concert. And I say that she who had never suspected the existence of the real me, suspected it then, when we glanced at each other across the breakfast-room. Upon these apparent trifles life swings, as upon a pivot, into new directions.

I sat with my aunt while Lucy went with the note. She returned soon with the reply, and the reply was:

'So sorry I can't accept your kind invitation. I should have liked to go awfully. But Fred has got the toothache, and I must not leave him.'

The toothache! And my very life, so it seemed to me, hung in the balance.

I did not hesitate one second.

'Hurrah!' I cried. 'She can go. I am to call for her in the cab.'

And I crushed the note cruelly, and threw it in the fire.

'Tell him to call at Ryleys',' I said to Rebecca as she was putting me and my dress into the cab.

And she told the cabman with that sharp voice of hers, always arrogant towards inferiors, to call at Ryleys.'

I put my head out of the cab window as soon as we were in

Oldcastle Street.

'Drive straight to Hanbridge,' I ordered.

The thing was done.

II

He was like his photograph, but the photograph had given me only the most inadequate idea of him. The photograph could not render his extraordinary fairness, nor the rich gold of his hair, nor the blue of his dazzling eyes. The first impression was that he was too beautiful for a man, that he had a woman's beauty, that he had the waxen beauty of a doll; but the firm, decisive lines of the mouth and chin, the overhanging brows, and the luxuriance of his amber moustache, spoke more sternly. Gradually one perceived that beneath the girlish mask, beneath the contours and the complexion incomparably delicate, there was an individuality intensely and provocatively male. His body was rather less than tall, and it was muscular and springy. He walked on to the platform as an unspoilt man should walk, and he bowed to the applause as if bowing chivalrously to a woman whom he respected but did not love. Diaz was twenty-six that year; he had recently returned from a tour round the world; he was filled full of triumph, renown, and adoration. As I have said, he was already legendary. He had become so great and so marvellous that those who had never seen him were in danger of forgetting that he was a living human being, obliged to eat and drink, and practise scales, and visit his tailor's. Thus it had happened to me. During the first moments I found myself thinking, 'This cannot be Diaz. It is not true that at last I see him. There must be some mistake.' Then he sat down leisurely to the piano; his gaze ranged across the hall, and I fancied that, for a second, it met mine. My two seats were in the first row of the stalls, and I could see every slightest change of his face. So that at length I felt that Diaz was real, and that he was really there close in front of me, a seraph and yet very human. He was all alone on the great platform, and the ebonized piano seemed enormous and formidable before him. And all around was the careless public—ignorant, unsympathetic, exigent, impatient, even inimical—two thousand persons who would get value for their money or know the reason why. The electric light and the inclement gaze of society rained down cruelly upon that defenceless head. I wanted to protect it. The tears rose to my eyes, and I stretched out towards Diaz the hands of my soul. My passionate sympathy must have reached him like a beneficent influence, of which, despite the perfect self-possession and self-confidence of his demeanour, it seemed to me that he had need.

I had risked much that night. I had committed an enormity. No one but a grown woman who still vividly remembers her girlhood can appreciate my feelings as I drove from Bursley to Hanbridge in the cab, and as I got out of the cab in the crowd, and gave up my ticket, and entered the glittering auditorium of the Jubilee Hall. I was alone, at night, in the public places, under the eye of the world. And I was guiltily alone. Every fibre of my body throbbed with the daring and the danger and the romance of the adventure. The horror of revealing the truth to Aunt Constance, as I was bound to do—of telling her that I had lied, and that I had left my maiden's modesty behind in my bedroom, gripped me at intervals like some appalling and exquisite instrument of torture. And yet, ere Diaz had touched the piano with his broad white hand, I was content, I was rewarded, and I was justified.

The programme began with Chopin's first Ballade.

There was an imperative summons, briefly sustained, which developed into an appeal and an invocation, ascending, falling, and still higher ascending, till it faded and expired, and then, after a little pause, was revived; then silence, and two chords, defining and clarifying the vagueness of the appeal and the invocation. And then, almost before I was aware of it, there stole forth from under the fingers of Diaz the song of the soul of man, timid, questioning, plaintive, neither sad nor joyous, but simply human, seeking what it might find on earth. The song changed subtly from mood to mood, expressing that which nothing but itself could express; and presently there was a low and gentle menace, thrice repeated under the melody of the song, and the reply of the song was a proud cry, a haughty contempt of these furtive warnings, and a sudden winged leap into the empyrean towards the Eternal Spirit. And then the melody was lost in a depth, and the song became turgid and wild and wilder, hysteric, irresolute, frantically groping, until at last it found its peace and its salvation. And the treasure was veiled in a mist of arpeggios, but one by one these were torn away, and there was a hush, a pause, and a preparation; and the soul of man broke into a new song of what it had found on earth—the magic of the tenderness of love—an air so caressing and so sweet, so calmly happy and so mournfully sane, so bereft of illusions and so naïve, that it seemed to reveal in a few miraculous phrases the secret intentions of God. It was too beautiful; it told me too much about myself; it vibrated my nerves to such an unbearable spasm of pleasure that I might have died had I not willed to live.... It gave place momentarily to the song of the question and the search, but only to return, and to return again, with a more thrilling and glorious assurance. It was drowned in doubt, but it emerged triumphantly, covered with noble and delicious ornaments, and swimming strongly on mysterious waves. And finally, with speed and with fire, it was transformed and caught up into the last ecstasy, the ultimate passion. The soul swept madly between earth and heaven, fell, rose; and there was a dreadful halt. Then a loud blast, a distortion of the magic, an upward rush, another and a louder blast, and a thunderous fall, followed by two massive and terrifying chords....

Diaz was standing up and bowing to his public. What did they understand? Did they understand anything? I cannot tell. But I know that they felt. A shudder of feeling had gone through the hall. It was in vain that people tried to emancipate themselves from the spell by the violence of their applause. They could not. We were all together under the enchantment. Some may have seen clearly, some darkly, but we were equal before the throne of that mighty enchanter. And the enchanter bowed and bowed with a grave, sympathetic smile, and then disappeared. I had not clapped my hands; I had not moved. Only my full eyes had followed him as he left the platform; and when he returned—because the applause would not cease—my eyes watched over him as he came back to the centre of the platform. He stood directly in front of me, smiling more gaily now. And suddenly our glances met! Yes; I could not be mistaken. They met, and mine held his for several seconds.... Diaz had looked at me. Diaz had singled me out from the crowd. I blushed hotly, and I was conscious of a surpassing joy. My spirit was transfigured. I knew that such a man was above kings. I knew that the world and everything of loveliness that it contained was his. I knew that he moved like a beautiful god through the groves of delight, and that what he did was right, and whom he beckoned came, and whom he touched was blessed. And my eyes had held his eyes for a little space.

The enchantment deepened. I had read that the secret of playing Chopin had died with Chopin; but I felt sure that evening, as I have felt sure since, that Chopin himself, aristocrat of the soul as he was, would have received Diaz as an equal, might even have acknowledged in him a superior. For Diaz had a physique, and he had a mastery, a tyranny, of the keyboard that Chopin could not have possessed. Diaz had come to the front in a generation of pianists who had lifted technique to a plane of which neither Liszt nor Rubinstein dreamed. He had succeeded primarily by his gigantic and incredible technique. And then, when his technique had astounded the world, he had invited the world to forget it, as the glass is forgotten through which is seen beauty. And Diaz's gift was now such that there appeared to intervene nothing between his conception of the music and the strings of the piano, so perfected was the mechanism. Difficulties had ceased to exist.

The performance of some pianists is so wonderful that it seems as if they were crossing Niagara on a tight-rope, and you tremble lest they should fall off. It was not so with Diaz. When Diaz played you experienced the pure emotions caused by the unblurred contemplation of that beauty which the great masters had created, and which Diaz had tinted with the rare dyes of his personality. You forgot all but beauty. The piano was not a piano; it was an Arabian magic beyond physical laws, and it, too, had a soul.

So Diaz laid upon us the enchantment of Chopin and of himself. Mazurkas, nocturnes, waltzes, scherzos, polonaises, preludes, he exhibited to us in groups those manifestations of that supreme spirit— that spirit at once stern and tender, not more sad than joyous, and always sane, always perfectly balanced, always preoccupied with beauty. The singular myth of a Chopin decadent, weary, erratic, mournful, hysterical, at odds with fate, was completely dissipated; and we perceived instead the grave artist nourished on Bach and studious in form, and the strong soul that had dared to look on life as it is, and had found beauty everywhere. Ah! how the air trembled and glittered with visions! How melody and harmony filled every corner of the hall with the silver and gold of sound! How the world was changed out of recognition! How that which had seemed unreal became real, and that which had seemed real receded to a horizon remote and fantastic!...

He was playing the fifteenth Prelude in D flat now, and the water was dropping, dropping ceaselessly on the dead body, and the beautiful calm song rose serenely in the dream, and then lost itself amid the presaging chords of some sinister fate, and came again, exquisite and fresh as ever, and then was interrupted by a high note like a clarion; and while Diaz held that imperious, compelling note, he turned his face slightly from the piano and gazed at me. Several times since the first time our eyes had met, by accident as I thought. But this was a deliberate seeking on his part. Again I flushed hotly. Again I had the terrible shudder of joy. I feared for a moment lest all the Five Towns was staring at me, thus singled out by Diaz; but it was not so: I had the wit to perceive that no one could remark me as the recipient of that hurried and burning glance. He had half a dozen bars to play, yet his eyes did not leave mine, and I would not let mine leave his. He remained moveless while the last chord expired, and then it seemed to me that his gaze had gone further, had passed through me into some unknown. The applause startled him to his feet.

My thought was: 'What can he be thinking of me?... But hundreds of women must have loved him!'

In the interval an attendant came on to the platform and altered the position of the piano. Everybody asked: 'What's that for?' For the new position was quite an unusual one; it brought the tail of the piano nearer to the audience, and gave a better view of the keyboard to the occupants of the seats in the orchestra behind the platform. 'It's a question of the acoustics, that's what it is,' observed a man near me, and a woman replied: 'Oh, I see!'

When Diaz returned and seated himself to play the Berceuse, I saw that he could look at me without turning his head. And now, instead of flushing, I went cold. My spine gave way suddenly. I began to be afraid; but of what I was afraid I had not the least idea. I fixed my eyes on my programme as he launched into the Berceuse. Twice I glanced up, without, however, moving my head, and each time his burning blue eyes met mine. (But why did I choose moments when the playing of the piece demanded less than all his attention?) The Berceuse was a favourite. In sentiment it was simpler than the great pieces that had preceded it. Its excessive delicacy attracted; the finesse of its embroidery swayed and enraptured the audience; and the applause at the close was mad, deafening, and peremptory. But Diaz was notorious as a refuser of encores. It had been said that he would see a hall wrecked by an angry mob before he would enlarge his programme. Four times he came forward and acknowledged the tribute, and four times he went back. At the fifth response he halted directly in front of me, and in his bold, grave eyes I saw a question. I saw it, and I would not answer. If he had spoken aloud to me I could not have more clearly understood. But I would not answer. And then some power within myself, hitherto unsuspected by me, some natural force, took possession of me, and I nodded my head.... Diaz went to the piano.

He hesitated, brushing lightly the keys.

'The Prelude in F sharp,' my thought ran. 'If he would play that!'

And instantly he broke into that sweet air, with its fateful hushed accompaniment—the trifle which Chopin threw off in a moment of his highest inspiration.

'It is the thirteenth Prelude,' I reflected. I was disturbed, profoundly troubled.

The next piece was the last, and it was the Fantasia, the masterpiece of Chopin.

In the Fantasia there speaks the voice of a spirit which has attained all that humanity may attain: of wisdom, of power, of pride and glory. And now it is like the roll of an army marching slowly through terrific defiles; and now it is like the quiet song of royal wanderers meditating in vast garden landscapes, with mossy masonry and long pools and cypresses, and a sapphire star shining in the purple sky on the shoulder of a cypress; and now it is like the cry of a lost traveller, who, plunging heavily through a virgin forest, comes suddenly upon a green circular sward, smooth as a carpet, with an antique statue of a beautiful nude girl in the midst; and now it is like the oratory of richly-gowned philosophers awaiting death in gorgeous and gloomy palaces; and now it is like the upward rush of winged things that are determined to achieve, knowing well the while that the ecstasy of longing is better than the assuaging of desire. And though the voice of this spirit speaking in the music disguises itself so variously, it is always the same. For it cannot, and it would not, hide the strange and rare timbre which distinguishes it from all others—that quality which springs from a pure and calm vision, of life. The voice of this spirit says that it has lost every illusion about life, and that life seems only the more beautiful. It says that activity is but another form of contemplation, pain but another form of pleasure, power but another form of weakness, hate but another form of love, and that it is well these things should be so. It says there is no end, only a means; and that the highest joy is to suffer, and the supreme wisdom is to exist. If you will but live, it cries, that grave but yet passionate voice—if you will but live! Were there a heaven, and you reached it, you could do no more than live. The true heaven is here where you live, where you strive and lose, and weep and laugh. And the true hell is here, where you forget to live, and blind your eyes to the omnipresent and terrible beauty of existence....

No, no; I cannot—I cannot describe further the experiences of my soul while Diaz played. When words cease, music has scarcely begun. I know now—I did not know it then—that Diaz was playing as perhaps he had never played before. The very air was charged with exquisite emotion, which went in waves across the hall, changing and blanching faces, troubling hearts, and moistening eyes.... And then he finished. It was over. In every trembling breast was a pang of regret that this spell, this miracle, this divine revolution, could not last into eternity.... He stood bowing, one hand touching the piano. And as the revolution he had accomplished in us was divine, so was he divine. I felt, and many another woman in the audience felt, that no reward could be too great for the beautiful and gifted creature who had entranced us and forced us to see what alone in life was worth seeing: that the whole world should be his absolute dominion; that his happiness should be the first concern of mankind; that if a thousand suffered in order to make him happy for a moment, it mattered not; that laws were not for him; that if he sinned, his sin must not be called a sin, and that he must be excused from remorse and from any manner of woe.

The applauding multitude stood up, and moved slightly towards the exits, and then stopped, as if ashamed of this readiness to desert the sacred temple. Diaz came forward three times, and each time the applause increased to a tempest; but he only smiled—smiled gravely. I could not see distinctly whether his eyes had sought mine, for mine were full of tears. No persuasions could induce him to show himself a fourth time, and at length a middle-aged man appeared and stated that Diaz was extremely gratified by his reception, but that he was also extremely exhausted and had left the hall.

We departed, we mortals; and I was among the last to leave the auditorium. As I left the lights were being extinguished over the platform, and an attendant was closing the piano. The foyer was crowded with people waiting to get out. The word passed that it was raining heavily. I wondered how I should find my cab. I felt very lonely and unknown; I was overcome with sadness—with a sense of the futility and frustration of my life. Such is the logic of the soul, and such the force of reaction. Gradually the foyer emptied.

III

'You think I am happy,' said Diaz, gazing at me with a smile suddenly grave; 'but I am not. I seek something which I cannot find. And my playing is only a relief from the fruitless search; only that. I am forlorn.'

'You!' I exclaimed, and my eyes rested on his, long.

Yes, we had met. Perhaps it had been inevitable since the beginning of time that we should meet; but it was none the less amazing. Perhaps I had inwardly known that we should meet; but, none the less, I was astounded when a coated and muffled figure came up swiftly to me in the emptying foyer, and said: 'Ah! you are here! I cannot leave without thanking you for your sympathy. I have never before felt such sympathy while playing.' It was a golden voice, pitched low, and the words were uttered with a very slight foreign accent, which gave them piquancy. I could not reply; something rose in my throat, and the caressing voice continued: 'You are pale. Do you feel ill? What can I do? Come with me to the artists' room; my secretary is there.' I put out a hand gropingly, for I could not see clearly, and I thought I should reel and fall. It touched his shoulder. He took my arm, and we went; no one had noticed us, and I had not spoken a word. In the room to which he guided me, through a long and sombre corridor, there was no sign of a secretary. I drank some water. 'There, you are better!' he cried. 'Thank you,' I said, but scarcely whispering. 'How fortunate I ventured to come to you just at that moment! You might have fallen'; and he smiled again. I shook my head. I said: 'It was your coming—that—that—made me dizzy!' 'I profoundly regret—' he began. 'No, no,' I interrupted him; and in that instant I knew I was about to say something which society would, justifiably, deem unpardonable in a girl situated as I was. 'I am so glad you came'; and I smiled, courageous and encouraging. For once in my life—for the first time in my adult life—I determined to be my honest self to another. 'Your voice is exquisitely beautiful,' he murmured. I thrilled.

Of what use to chronicle the steps, now halting, now only too hasty, by which our intimacy progressed in that gaunt and echoing room? He asked me no questions as to my identity. He just said that he would like to play to me in private if that would give me pleasure, and that possibly I could spare an hour and would go with him.... Afterwards his brougham would be at my disposal. His tone was the perfection of deferential courtesy. Once the secretary came in—a young man rather like himself—and they talked together in a foreign language that was not French nor German; then the secretary bowed and retired.... We were alone.... There can be no sort of doubt that unless I was prepared to flout the wisdom of the ages, I ought to have refused his suggestion. But is not the wisdom of the ages a medicine for majorities? And, indeed, I was prepared to flout it, as in our highest and our lowest moments we often are. Moreover, how many women in my place, confronted by that divine creature, wooed by that wondrous personality, intoxicated by that smile and that voice, allured by the appeal of those marvellous hands, would have found the strength to resist? I did not resist, I yielded; I accepted. I was already in disgrace with Aunt Constance—as well be drowned in twelve feet of water as in six!

So we drove rapidly away in the brougham, through the miry, light-reflecting streets of Hanbridge in the direction of Knype. And the raindrops ran down the windows of the brougham, and in the cushioned interior we could see each other darkly. He did his best to be at ease, and he almost succeeded. My feeling towards him, as regards the external management, the social guidance, of the affair, was as though we were at sea in a dangerous storm, and he was on the bridge and I was a mere passenger, and could take no responsibility. Who knew through what difficult channels we might not have to steer, and from what lee-shores we might not have to beat away? I saw that he perceived this. When I offered him some awkward compliment about his good English, he seized the chance of a narrative, and told me about his parentage: how his mother was Scotch, and his father Danish, and how, after his father's death, his mother had married Emilio Diaz, a Spanish teacher of music in Edinburgh, and how he had taken, by force of early habit, the name of his stepfather. The whole world was familiar with these facts, and I was familiar with them; but their recital served our turn in the brougham, and, of course, Diaz could add touches which had escaped the *Staffordshire Recorder*, and perhaps all other papers. He was explaining to me that his secretary was his stepfather's son by another wife, when we arrived at the Five Towns Hotel, opposite Knype Railway Station. I might have foreseen that that would be our destination. I hooded myself as well as I could, and followed him quickly to the first-floor. I sank down into a chair nearly breathless in his sitting-room, and he took my cloak, and then poked the bright fire that was burning. On a small table were some glasses and a decanter, and a few sandwiches. I surmised that the secretary had been before us and arranged things, and discreetly departed. My adventure appeared to me suddenly and over-poweringly in its full enormity. 'Oh,' I sighed, 'if I were a man like you!' Then it was that, gazing up at me from the fire, Diaz had said that he was not happy, that he was forlorn.

'Yes,' he proceeded, sitting down and crossing his legs; 'I am profoundly dissatisfied. What is my life? Eight or nine months in the year it is a homeless life of hotels and strange faces and strange pianos. You do not know how I hate a strange piano. That one'—he pointed to a huge instrument which had evidently been placed in the room specially for him—'is not very bad; but I made its acquaintance only yesterday, and after to-morrow I shall never see it again. I wander across the world, and everybody I meet looks at me as if I ought to be in a museum, and bids me make acquaintance with a strange piano.'

'But have you no friends?' I ventured.

'Who can tell?' he replied. 'If I have, I scarcely ever see them.'

'And no home?'

'I have a home on the edge of the forest of Fontainebleau, and I loathe it.'

'Why do you loathe it?'

'Ah! For what it has witnessed—for what it has witnessed.' He sighed.

'Suppose we discuss something else.'

You must remember my youth, my inexperience, my lack of adroitness in social intercourse. I talked quietly and slowly, like my aunt, and I know that I had a tremendous air of sagacity and self-possession; but beneath that my brain and heart were whirling, bewildered in a delicious, dazzling haze of novel sensations. It was not I who spoke, but a new being, excessively perturbed into a consciousness of new powers. I said:

'You say you are friendless, but I wonder how many women are dying for love of you.'

He started. There was a pause. I felt myself blushing.

'Let me guess at your history,' he said. 'You have lived much alone with your thoughts, and you have read a great deal of the finest romantic poetry, and you have been silent, especially with men. You have seen little of men.'

'But I understand them,' I answered boldly.

'I believe you do,' he admitted; and he laughed. 'So I needn't explain to you that a thousand women dying of love for one man will not help that man to happiness, unless he is dying of love for the thousand and first.'

'And have you never loved?'

The words came of themselves out of my mouth.

'I have deceived myself—in my quest of sympathy,' he said.

'Can you be sure that, in your quest of sympathy, you are not deceiving yourself tonight?'

'Yes,' he cried quickly, 'I can.' And he sprang up and almost ran to the piano. 'You remember the D flat Prelude?' he said, breaking into the latter part of the air, and looking at me the while. 'When I came to that note and caught your gaze'—he struck the B flat and held it—'I knew that I had found sympathy. I knew it! I knew it! I knew it! Do you remember?'

'Remember what?'

'The way we looked at each other.'

'Yes,' I breathed, 'I remember.'

'How can I thank you? How can I thank you?'

He seemed to be meditating. His simplicity, his humility, his kindliness were more than I could bear.

'Please do not speak like that,' I entreated him, pained. 'You are the greatest artist in the world, and I am nobody—nobody at all. I do not know why I am here. I cannot imagine what you have seen in me. Everything is a mystery. All I feel is that I am in your presence, and that I am not worthy to be. No matter how long I live, I shall never experience again the joy that I have now. But if you talk about thanking me, I must run away, because I cannot stand it—and—and—you haven't played for me, and you said you would.'

He approached me, and bent his head towards mine, and I glanced up through a mist and saw his eyes and the short, curly auburn locks on his forehead.

'The most beautiful things, and the most vital things, and the most lasting things,' he said softly, 'are often mysterious and inexplicable and sudden. And let me tell you that you do not know how lovely you are. You do not know the magic of your voice, nor the grace of your gestures. But time and man will teach you. What shall I play?'

He was very close to me.

'Bach,' I ejaculated, pointing impatiently to the piano.

I fancied that Bach would spread peace abroad in my soul.

He resumed his place at the piano, and touched the keys.

'Another thing that makes me more sure that I am not deceiving myself to-night,' he said, taking his fingers off the keys, but staring at the keyboard, 'is that you have not regretted coming here. You have not called yourself a wicked woman. You have not even accused me of taking advantage of your innocence.'

And ere I could say a word he had begun the Chromatic Fantasia, smiling faintly.

And I had hoped for peace from Bach! I had often suspected that deep passion was concealed almost everywhere within the restraint and the apparent calm of Bach's music, but the full force of it had not been shown to me till this glorious night. Diaz' playing was tenfold more impressive, more effective, more revealing in the hotel parlour than in the great hall. The Chromatic Fantasia seemed as full of the magnificence of life as that other Fantasia which he had given an hour or so earlier. Instead of peace I had the whirlwind; instead of tranquillity a riot; instead of the poppy an alarming potion. The rendering was masterly to the extreme of masterliness.

When he had finished I rose and passed to the fireplace in silence; he did not stir.

'Do you always play like that?' I asked at length.

'No,' he said; 'only when you are there. I have never played the Chopin Fantasia as I played it to-night. The Chopin was all right; but do not be under any illusion: what you have just heard is Bach played by a Chopin player.'

Then he left the piano and went to the small table where the glasses were.

'You must be in need of refreshment,' he whispered gaily. 'Nothing is more exhausting than listening to the finest music.'

'It is you who ought to be tired,' I replied; 'after that long concert, to be playing now.'

'I have the physique of a camel,' he said. 'I am never tired so long as I am sure of my listeners. I would play for you till breakfast to-morrow.'

The decanter contained a fluid of a pleasant green tint. He poured very carefully this fluid to the depth of half an inch in one glass and three-quarters of an inch in another glass. Then he filled both glasses to the brim with water, accomplishing the feat with infinite pains and enjoyment, as though it had been part of a ritual.

'There!' he said, offering me in his steady hand the glass which had received the smaller quantity of the green fluid. 'Taste.'

'But what is it?' I demanded.

'Taste,' he repeated, and he himself tasted.

I obeyed. At the first mouthful I thought the liquid was somewhat sinister and disagreeable, but immediately afterwards I changed my opinion, and found it ingratiating, enticing, and stimulating, and yet not strong.

'Do you like it?' he asked.

I nodded, and drank again.

'It is wonderful,' I answered. 'What do you call it?'

'Men call it absinthe,' he said.

'But—'

I put the glass on the mantelpiece and picked it up again.

'Don't be frightened,' he soothed me. 'I know what you were going to say. You have always heard that absinthe is the deadliest of all poisons, that it is the curse of Paris, and that it makes the most terrible of all drunkards. So it is; so it does. But not as we are drinking it; not as I invariably drink it.'

'Of course,' I said, proudly confident in him. 'You would not have offered it to me otherwise.'

'Of course I should not,' he agreed. 'I give you my word that a few drops of absinthe in a tumbler of water make the most effective and the least harmful stimulant in the world.'

'I am sure of it,' I said.

'But drink slowly,' he advised me.

I refused the sandwiches. I had no need of them. I felt sufficient unto myself. I no longer had any apprehension. My body, my brain, and my soul seemed to be at the highest pitch of efficiency. The fear of being maladroit departed from me. Ideas—delicate and subtle ideas—welled up in me one after another; I was bound to give utterance to them. I began to talk about my idol Chopin, and I explained to Diaz my esoteric interpretation of the Fantasia. He was sitting down now, but I still stood by the fire.

'Yes, he said, 'that is very interesting.'

'What does the Fantasia mean to you?' I asked him.

'Nothing,' he said.

'Nothing!'

'Nothing, in the sense you wish to convey. Everything, in another sense. You can attach any ideas you please to music, but music, if you will forgive me saying so, rejects them all equally. Art has to do with emotions, not with ideas, and the great defect of literature is that it can only express emotions by means of ideas. What makes music the greatest of all the arts is that it can express emotions without ideas. Literature can appeal to the soul only through the mind. Music goes direct. Its language is a language which the soul alone understands, but which the soul can never translate. Therefore all I can say of the Fantasia is that it moves me profoundly. I *know how* it moves me, but I cannot tell you; I cannot even tell myself.'

Vistas of comprehension opened out before me.

'Oh, do go on,' I entreated him. 'Tell me more about music. Do you not think Chopin the greatest composer that ever lived? You must do, since you always play him.'

He smiled.

'No,' he said, 'I do not. For me there is no supremacy in art. When fifty artists have contrived to be supreme, supremacy becomes impossible. Take a little song by Grieg. It is perfect, it is supreme. No one could be greater than Grieg was great when he wrote that song. The whole last act of *The Twilight of the Gods* is not greater than a little song of Grieg's.'

'I see,' I murmured humbly. '*The Twilight of the Gods*—that is Wagner, isn't it?'

'Yes. Don't you know your Wagner?'

'No. I—'

'You don't know *Tristan*?'

He jumped up, excited.

'How could I know it?' I expostulated. 'I have never seen any opera. I know the marches from *Tannhäuser* and *Lohengrin*, and "O Star of Eve!"'

'But it is impossible that you don't know *Tristan*!' he exclaimed. 'The second act of *Tristan* is the greatest piece of love-music—No, it isn't.' He laughed. 'I must not contradict myself. But it is marvellous—marvellous! You know the story?'

'Yes,' I said. 'Play me some of it.'

'I will play the Prelude,' he answered.

I gulped down the remaining drops in my glass and crossed the room to a chair where I could see his face. And he played the Prelude to the most passionately voluptuous opera ever written. It was my first real introduction to Wagner, my first glimpse of that enchanted field. I was ravished, rapt away.

'Wagner was a great artist in spite of himself,' said Diaz, when he had finished. 'He assigned definite and precise ideas to all those melodies. Nothing could be more futile. I shall not label them for you. But perhaps you can guess the love-motive for yourself.'

'Yes, I can,' I said positively. 'It is this.'

I tried to hum the theme, but my voice refused obedience. So I came to the piano, and played the theme high up in the treble, while Diaz was still sitting on the piano-stool. I trembled even to touch the piano in his presence; but I did it.

'You have guessed right,' he said; and then he asked me in a casual tone:

'Do you ever play pianoforte duets?'

'Often,' I replied unsuspectingly, 'with my aunt. We play the symphonies of Beethoven, Mozart, Schubert, Haydn, and overtures, and so on.'

'Awfully good fun, isn't it?' he smiled.

'Splendid!' I said.

'I've got *Tristan* here arranged for pianoforte duet,' he said. 'Tony, my secretary, enjoys playing it. You shall play part of the second act with me.'

'Me! With you!'

'Certainly.'

'Impossible! I should never dare! How do you know I can play at all?'

'You have just proved it to me,' said he. 'Come; you will not refuse me this!'

I wanted to leave the vicinity of the piano. I felt that, once out of the immediate circle of his tremendous physical influence, I might manage to escape the ordeal which he had suggested. But I could not go away. The silken nets of his personality had been cast, and I was enmeshed. And if I was happy, it was with a dreadful happiness.

'But, really, I can't play with you,' I said weakly.

His response was merely to look up at me over his shoulder. His beautiful face was so close to mine, and it expressed such a naïve and strong yearning for my active and intimate sympathy, and such divine frankness, and such perfect kindliness, that I had no more will to resist. I knew I should suffer horribly in spoiling by my coarse amateurishness the miraculous finesse of his performance, but I resigned myself to suffering. I felt towards him as I had felt during the concert: that he must have his way at no matter what cost, that he had already earned the infinite gratitude of the entire world—in short, I raised him in my soul to a god's throne; and I accepted humbly the great, the incredible honour he did me. And I was right—a thousand times right.

And in the same moment he was like a charming child to me: such is always in some wise the relation between the creature born to enjoy and the creature born to suffer.

'I'll try,' I said; 'but it will be appalling.'

I laughed and shook my head.

'We shall see how appalling it will be,' he murmured, as he got the volume of music.

He fetched a chair for me, and we sat down side by side, he on the stool and I on the chair.

'I'm afraid my chair is too low,' I said.

'And I'm sure this stool is too high,' he said. 'Suppose we exchange.'

So we both rose to change the positions of the chair and the stool, and our garments touched and almost our faces, and at that very moment there was a loud rap at the door.

I darted away from him.

'What's that?' I cried, low in a fit of terror.

'Who's there?' he called quietly; but he did not stir.

We gazed at each other.

The knock was repeated, sharply and firmly.

'Who's there?' Diaz demanded again.

'Go to the door,' I whispered.

He hesitated, and then we heard footsteps receding down the corridor. Diaz went slowly to the door, opened it wide, slipped out into the corridor, and looked into the darkness.

'Curious!' he commented tranquilly. 'I see no one.'

He came back into the room and shut the door softly, and seemed thereby to shut us in, to enclose us against the world in a sweet domesticity of our own. The fire was burning brightly, the glasses and the decanter on the small table spoke of cheer, the curtains were drawn, and through a half-open door behind the piano one had a hint of a mysterious other room; one could see nothing within it save a large brass knob or ball, which caught the light of the candle on the piano.

'You were startled,' he said. 'You must have a little more of our cordial—just a spoonful.'

He poured out for me an infinitesimal quantity, and the same for himself.

I sighed with relief as I drank. My terror left me. But the trifling incident had given me the clearest perception of what I was doing, and that did not leave me.

We sat down a second time to the piano.

'You understand,' he explained, staring absently at the double page of music, 'this is the garden scene. When the curtain goes up it is dark in the garden, and Isolda is there with her maid Brangaena. The king, her husband, has just gone off hunting—you will hear the horns dying in the distance—and Isolda is expecting her lover, Tristan. A torch is burning in the wall of the castle, and as soon as she gives him the signal by extinguishing it he comes to her. You will know the exact moment when they meet. Then there is the love-scene. Oh! when we arrive at that you will be astounded. You will hear the very heart-beats of the lovers. Are you ready?'

'Yes.'

We began to play. But it was ridiculous. I knew it would be ridiculous. I was too dazed, and artistically too intimidated, to read the notes. The notes danced and pranced before me. All I could see on my page was the big black letters at the top, 'Zweiter Aufzug.' And furthermore, on that first page both the theme and the accompaniment were in the bass of the piano. Diaz had scarcely anything to do. I threw up my hands and closed my eyes.

'I can't,' I whispered, 'I can't. I would if I could.'

He gently took my hand.

'My dear companion,' he said, 'tell me your name.'

I was surprised. Memories of the Bible, for some inexplicable reason, flashed through my mind.

'Magdalen,' I replied, and my voice was so deceptively quiet and sincere that he believed it.

I could see that he was taken aback.

'It is a holy name and a good name,' he said, after a pause. 'Magda, you are perfectly capable of reading this music with me, and you will read it, won't you? Let us begin afresh. Leave the accompaniment with me, and play the theme only. Further on it gets easier.'

And in another moment we were launched on that sea so strange to me. The influence of Diaz over me was complete. Inspired by his will, I had resolved intensely to read the music correctly and sympathetically, and lo! I was succeeding! He turned the page with the incredible rapidity and dexterity of which only great pianists seem to have the secret, and in conjunction with my air in the bass he was suddenly, magically, drawing out from the upper notes the sweetest and most intoxicating melody I had ever heard. The exceeding beauty of the thing laid hold on me, and I abandoned myself to it. I felt sure now that, at any rate, I should not disgrace myself.'

'Unless it was Chopin,' whispered Diaz. 'No one could ever see two things at once as well as Wagner.'

We surged on through the second page. Again the lightning turn of the page, and then the hunters' horns were heard departing from the garden of love, receding, receding, until they subsided into a scarce-heard drone, out of which rose another air. And as the sound of the horns died away, so died away all my past and all my solicitudes for the future. I surrendered utterly and passionately to the spell of the beauty which we were opening like a long scroll. I had ceased to suffer.

The absinthe and Diaz had conjured a spirit in me which was at once feverish and calm. I was reading at sight difficult music full of modulations and of colour, and I was reading it with calm assurance of heart and brain. Deeper down the fever raged, but so separately that I might have had two individualities. Enchanted as I was by the rich and complex concourse of melodies which ascended from the piano and swam about our heads, this fluctuating tempest of sound was after all only a background for the emotions to which it gave birth in me. Naturally they were the emotions of love—the sense of the splendour of love, the headlong passion of love, the transcendent carelessness of love, the finality of love. I saw in love the sole and sacred purpose of the universe, and my heart whispered, with a new import: 'Where love is, there is God also.'

The fever of the music increased, and with it my fever. We seemed to be approaching some mighty climax. I thought I might faint with ecstasy, but I held on, and the climax arrived—a climax which touched the limits of expression in expressing all that two souls could feel in coming together.

'Tristan has come into the garden,' I muttered.

And Diaz, turning his face towards me, nodded.

We plunged forward into the love-scene itself—the scene in which the miracle of love is solemnized and celebrated. I thought that of all miracles, the miracle which had occurred that night, and was even then occurring, might be counted among the most wondrous. What occult forces, what secret influences of soul on soul, what courage on his part, what sublime immodesty and unworldliness on mine had brought it about! In what dreadful disaster would it not end! ... I cared not in that marvellous hectic hour how it would end. I knew I had been blessed beyond the common lot of women. I knew that I was living more intensely and more fully than I could have hoped to live. I knew that my experience was a supreme experience, and that another such could not be contained in my life.... And Diaz was so close, so at one with me.... A hush descended on the music, and I found myself playing strange disturbing chords with the left hand, irregularly repeated, opposing the normal accent of the bar, and becoming stranger and more disturbing. And Diaz was playing an air fragmentary and poignant. The lovers were waiting; the very atmosphere of the garden was drenched with an agonizing and exquisite anticipation. The whole world stood still, expectant, while the strange chords fought gently and persistently against the rhythm.

'Hear the beating of their hearts,' Diaz' whisper floated over the chords.

It was too much. The obsession of his presence, reinforced by the vibrating of his wistful, sensuous voice, overcame me suddenly. My hands fell from the keyboard. He looked at me—and with what a glance!

'I can bear no more,' I cried wildly. 'It is too beautiful, too beautiful!'

And I rushed from the piano, and sat down in an easy-chair, and hid my face in my hands.

He came to me, and bent over me.

'Magda,' he whispered, 'show me your face.' With his hands he delicately persuaded my hands away from my face, and forced me to look on him. 'How dark and splendid you are, Magda!' he said, still holding my hands. 'How humid and flashing your eyes! And those eyelashes, and that hair—dark, dark! And that bosom, with its rise and fall! And that low, rich voice, that is like dark wine! And that dress—dark, and full of mysterious shadows, like our souls! Magda, we must have known each other in a previous life. There can be no other explanation. And this moment is the fulfilment of that other life, which was not aroused. You were to be mine. You are mine, Magda!'

There is a fatalism in love. I felt it then. I had been called by destiny to give happiness, perhaps for a lifetime, but perhaps only for a brief instant, to this noble and glorious creature, on whom the gods had showered all gifts. Could I shrink back from my fate? And had he not already given me far more than I could ever return? The conventions of society seemed then like sand, foolishly raised to imprison the resistless tide of ocean. Nature, after all, is eternal and unchangeable, and everywhere the same. The great and solemn fact for me was that we were together, and he held me while our burning pulses throbbed in contact. He held me; he clasped me, and, despite my innocence, I knew at once that those hands were as expert to caress as to make music. I was proud and glad that he was not clumsy, that he was a master. And at that point I ceased to have volition....

IV

When I woke up, perplexed at first, but gradually remembering where I was, and what had occurred to me, the realistic and uncompromising light of dawn had commenced its pitiless inquiry, and it fell on the brass knob, which I had noticed a few hours before, from the other room, and on another brass knob a few feet away. My eyes smarted; I had disconcerting sensations at the back of my head; my hair was brittle, and as though charged with a dull electricity; I was conscious of actual pain, and an incubus, crushing but intangible, lay heavily, like a physical weight, on my heart. After the crest of the wave the trough—it must be so; but how profound the instinct which complains! I listened. I could hear his faint, regular breathing. I raised myself carefully on one elbow and looked at him. He was as beautiful in sleep as in consciousness; his lips were slightly parted, his cheek exquisitely flushed, and nothing could disarrange that short, curly hair. He slept with the calmness of the natural innocent man, to whom the assuaging of desires brings only content.

I felt that I must go, and hastily, frantically. I could not face him when he woke; I should not have known what to say; I should have been abashed, timid, clumsy, unequal to myself. And, moreover, I had the egoist's deep need to be alone, to examine my soul, to understand it intimately and utterly. And, lastly, I wanted to pay the bill of pleasure at once. I could never tolerate credit; I was like my aunt in that. Therefore, I must go home and settle the account in some way. I knew not how; I knew only that the thing must be done. Diaz had nothing to do with that; it was not his affair, and I should have resented his interference. Ah! when I was in the bill-paying mood, how hard I could be, how stony, how blind! And that morning I was like a Malay running amok.

Think not that when I was ready to depart I stopped and stooped to give him a final tender kiss. I did not even scribble a word of adieu or of explanation. I stole away on tiptoe, without looking at him. This sounds brutal, but it is a truth of my life, and I am writing my life—at least, I am writing those brief hours of my existence during which I lived. I had always a sort of fierce courage; and as I had proved the courage of my passion in the night, so I proved the courage of my—not my remorse, not my compunction, not my regret—but of my intellectual honesty in the morning. Proud and vain words, perhaps. Who can tell? No matter what sympathies I alienate, I am bound to say plainly that, though I am passionate, I am not sentimental. I came to him out of the void, and I went from him into the void. He found me, and he lost me. Between the autumn sunset and the autumn sunrise he had learnt to know me well, but he did not know my name nor my history; he had no clue, no cord to pull me back.

I passed into the sitting-room, dimly lighted through the drawn curtains, and there was the score of *Tristan* open on the piano. Yes; and if I were the ordinary woman I would add that there also were the ashes in the cold grate, and so symbolize the bitterness of memory and bring about a pang. But I have never regretted what is past. The cinders of that fire were to me cinders of a fire and nothing more.

In the doorway I halted. To go into the corridor was like braving the blast of the world, and I hesitated. Possibly I hesitated for a very little thing. Only the women among you will guess it. My dress was dark and severe. I had a simple, dark cloak. But I had no hat. I had no hat, and the most important fact in the universe for me then was that I had no hat. My whole life was changed; my heart and mind were in the throes of a revolution. I dared not imagine what would happen between my aunt and me; but this deficiency in my attire distressed me more than all else. At the other end of the obscure corridor was a chambermaid kneeling down and washing the linoleum. Ah, maid! Would I not have exchanged fates with you, then! I walked boldly up to her. She seemed to be surprised, but she continued to wring out a cloth in her pail as she looked at me.

'What time is it, please?' I asked her.

'Better than half-past six, ma'am,' said she.

She was young and emaciated.

'Have you got a hat you can lend me? Or I'll buy it from you.'

'A hat, ma'am?'

'Yes, a hat,' I repeated impatiently. And I flushed. 'I must go out at once, and I've—I've no hat And I can't—'

It is extraordinary how in a crisis one's organism surprises one. I had thought I was calm and full of self-control, but I had almost no command over my voice.

'I've got a boat-shaped straw, ma'am, if that's any use to you,' said the girl kindly.

What she surmised or what she knew I could not say. But I have found out since in my travels, that hotel chambermaids lose their illusions early. At any rate her tone was kindly.

'Get it me, there's a good girl,' I entreated her.

And when she brought it, I drew out the imitation pearl pins and put them between my teeth, and jammed the hat on my head and skewered it savagely with the pins.

'Is that right?'

'It suits you better than it does me, ma'am, I do declare,' she said.

'Oh, ma'am, this is too much—I really couldn't!'

I had given her five shillings.

'Nonsense! I am very much obliged to you,' I whispered hurriedly, and ran off.

She was a good girl. I hope she has never suffered. And yet I would not like to think she had died of consumption before she knew what life meant.

I hastened from the hotel. A man in a blue waistcoat with shining black sleeves was moving a large cocoa-nut mat in the hall, and the pattern of the mat was shown in dust on the tiles where the mat had been. He glanced at me absently as I flitted past; I encountered no other person. The square between the hotel and the station was bathed in pure sunshine—such sunshine as reaches the Five Towns only after a rain-storm has washed the soot out of the air. I felt, for a moment, obscene in that sunshine; but I had another and a stronger feeling. Although there was not a soul in the square, I felt as if I was regarding the world and mankind with different eyes from those of yesterday. Then I knew nothing; to-day I knew everything—so it seemed to me. It seemed to me that I understood all sorts of vague, subtle things that I had not understood before; that I had been blind and now saw; that I had become kinder, more sympathetic, more human. What these things were that I understood, or thought I understood, I could not have explained. All I felt was that a radical change of attitude had occurred in me. 'Poor world!

Poor humanity! My heart melts for you!' Thus spoke my soul, pouring itself out. The very stone facings of the station and the hotel seemed somehow to be humanized and to need my compassion.

I walked with eyes downcast into the station. I had determined to take the train from Knype to Shawport, a distance of three miles, and then to walk up the hill from Shawport through Oldcastle Street to Bursley. I hoped that by such a route at such an hour, I should be unlikely to meet acquaintances, of whom, in any case, I had few. My hopes appeared to be well founded, for the large booking-hall at the station was thronged with a multitude entirely strange to me—workmen and workwomen and workgirls crowded the place. The first-class and second-class booking-windows were shut, and a long tail of muscular men, pale men, stout women, and thin women pushed to take tickets at the other window. I was obliged to join them, and to wait my turn amid the odour of corduroy and shawl, and the strong odour of humanity; my nostrils were peculiarly sensitive that morning. Some of the men had herculean arms and necks, and it was these who wore pieces of string tied round their trousers below the knee, disclosing the lines of their formidable calves. The women were mostly pallid and quiet. All carried cans, or satchels, or baskets; here and there a man swung lightly on his shoulder a huge bag of tools, which I could scarcely have raised from the ground. Everybody was natural, direct, and eager; and no one attempted to be genteel or refined; no one pretended that he did not toil with his hands for dear life. I anticipated that I should excite curiosity, but I did not. The people had a preoccupied, hurried air. Only at the window itself, when the ticket-clerk, having made me repeat my demand, went to a distant part of his lair to get my ticket, did I detect behind me a wave of impatient and inimical interest in this drone who caused delay to busy people.

It was the same on the up-platform, the same in the subway, and the same on the down-platform. I was plunged in a sea of real, raw life; but I could not mingle with it; I was a bit of manufactured lace on that full tide of nature. The porters cried in a different tone from what they employed when the London and Manchester expresses, and the polite trains generally, were alongside. They cried fraternally, rudely; they were at one with the passengers. I alone was a stranger.

'These are the folk! These are the basis of society, and the fountain of *our* wealth and luxury!' I thought; for I was just beginning, at that period, to be interested in the disquieting aspects of the social organism, and my ideas were hot and crude. I was aware of these people on paper, but now, for the first time, I realized the immense rush and sweep of their existence, their nearness to Nature, their formidable directness. They frightened me with their vivid humanity.

I could find no first-class carriage on the train, and I got into a compartment where there were several girls and one young man. The girls were evidently employed in the earthenware manufacture. Each had her dinner-basket. Most of them were extremely neat; one or two wore gloves. From the young man's soiled white jacket under his black coat, I gathered that he was an engineer. The train moved out of the station and left the platform nearly empty. I pictured the train, a long procession of compartments like ours, full of rough, natural, ungenteel people. None of my companions spoke; none gave me more than a passing glance. It was uncanny.

Still, the fundamental, cardinal quality of my adventure remained prominent in my being, and it gave me countenance among these taciturn, musing workgirls, who were always at grips with the realities of life. 'Ah,' I thought, 'you little know what I know! I may appear a butterfly, but I have learnt the secret meaning of existence. I am above you, beyond you, by my experience, and by my terrible situation, and by the turmoil in my heart!' And then, quite suddenly, I reflected that they probably knew all that I knew, that some of them might have forgotten more than I had ever learnt. I remembered an absorbing correspondence about the manners of the Five Towns in the columns of the *Staffordshire Recorder*—a correspondence which had driven Aunt Constance to conceal the paper after the second week. I guessed that they might smile at the simplicity of my heart could they see it. Meaning of existence! Why, they were reared in it! The naturalness of natural people and of natural acts struck me like a blow, and I withdrew, whipped, into myself. My adventure grew smaller. But I recalled its ecstasies. I dwelt on the romantic perfection of Diaz. It seemed to me amazing, incredible, that Diaz, the glorious and incomparable Diaz, had loved me—*me*! out of all the ardent, worshipping women that the world contained. I wondered if he had wakened up, and I felt sorry for him. So far, I had not decided how soon, if at all, I should communicate with him. My mind was incapable of reaching past the next few hours—the next hour.

We stopped at a station surrounded by the evidences of that tireless, unceasing, and tremendous manufacturing industry which distinguishes the Five Towns, and I was left alone in the compartment. The train rumbled on through a landscape of fiery furnaces, and burning slag-heaps, and foul canals reflecting great smoking chimneys, all steeped in the mild sunshine. Could the toil-worn agents of this never-ending and gigantic productiveness find time for love? Perhaps they loved quickly and forgot, like animals. Thoughts such as these lurked sinister and carnal, strange beasts in the jungle of my poor brain. Then the train arrived at Shawport, and I was obliged to get out. I say 'obliged,' because I violently wished not to get out. I wished to travel on in that train to some impossible place, where things were arranged differently.

The station clock showed only five minutes to seven. I was astounded. It seemed to me that all the real world had been astir and busy for hours. And this extraordinary activity went on every morning while Aunt Constance and I lay in our beds and thought well of ourselves.

I shivered, and walked quickly up the street. I had positively not noticed that I was cold. I had scarcely left the station before Fred Ryley appeared in front of me. I saw that his face was swollen. My heart stopped. Of course, he would tell Ethel.... He passed me sheepishly without stopping, merely raising his hat, and murmuring the singular words:

'We're both very, very sorry.'

What in the name of Heaven could they possibly know, he and Ethel? And what right had he to ...? Did he smile furtively? Fred Ryley had sometimes a strange smile. I reddened, angry and frightened.

The distance between the station and our house proved horribly short. And when I arrived in front of the green gates, and put my hand on the latch, I knew that I had formed no plan whatever. I opened the right-hand gate and entered the garden. The blinds were still down, and the house looked so decorous and innocent in its age. My poor aunt! What a night she must have been through! It was inconceivable that I should tell her what had happened to me. Indeed, under the windows of that house it seemed inconceivable that the thing had happened which had happened. Inconceivable! Grotesque! Monstrous!

But could I lie? Could I rise to the height of some sufficient and kindly lie?

A hand drew slightly aside the blind of the window over the porch. I sighed, and went wearily, in my boat-shaped straw, up the gravelled path to the door.

Rebecca met me at the door. It was so early that she had not yet put on an apron. She looked tired, as if she had not slept.

'Come in, miss,' she said weakly, holding open the door.

It seemed to me that I did not need this invitation from a servant.

'I suppose you've all been fearfully upset, wondering where I was,' I began, entering the hall.

My adventure appeared fantastically unreal to me in the presence of this buxom creature, whom I knew to be incapable of imagining anything one hundredth part so dreadful.

'No, miss; I wasn't upset on account of you. You're always so sensible like. You always know what to do. I knew as you must have stopped the night with friends in Hanbridge on account of the heavy rain, and perhaps that there silly cabman not turning up, and them tramcars all crowded; and, of course, you couldn't telegraph.'

This view that I was specially sagacious and equal to emergencies rather surprised me.

'But auntie?' I demanded, trembling.

'Oh, miss!' cried Rebecca, glancing timidly over her shoulder, 'I want you to come with me into the dining-room before you go upstairs.'

She snuffled.

In the dining-room I went at once to the window to draw up the blinds.

'Not that, not that!' Rebecca appealed, weeping. 'For pity's sake!' And she caught my hand.

I then noticed that Lucy was standing in the doorway, also weeping.

Rebecca noticed this too.

'Lucy, you go to your kitchen this minute,' she said sharply, and then turned to me and began to cry again. 'Miss Peel—how can I tell you?'

'Why do you call me Miss Peel?' I asked her.

But I knew why. The thing flashed over me instantly. My dear aunt was dead.

'You've got no aunt,' said Rebecca. 'My poor dear! And you at the concert!'

I dropped my head and my bosom on the bare mahogany table and cried. Never before, and never since, have I spilt such tears—hot, painful drops, distilled plenteously from a heart too crushed and torn.

'There, there!' muttered Rebecca. 'I wish I could have told you different—less cruel; but it wasn't in me to do it.'

'And she's lying upstairs this very moment all cold and stiff,' a wailing voice broke in.

It was Lucy, who could not keep herself away from us.

'Will you go to your kitchen, my girl!'

Rebecca drove her off. 'And the poor thing's not stiff either. Her poor body's as soft as if she was only asleep, and doctor says it will be for a day or two. It's like that when they're took off like that, he says. Oh, Miss Carlotta—'

'Tell me all about it before I go upstairs,' I said.

I had recovered.

'Your poor aunt went to bed just as soon as you were gone, miss,' said Rebecca. 'She would have it she was quite well, only tired. I took her up a cup of cocoa at ten o'clock, and she seemed all right, and then I sends Lucy to bed, and I sits up in the kitchen to wait for you. Not a sound from your poor aunt. I must have dropped asleep, miss, in my chair, and I woke up with a start like, and the kitchen clock was near on one. Thinks I, perhaps Miss Carlotta's been knocking and ringing all this time and me not heard, and I rushes to the front door. But of course you weren't there. The porch was nothing but a pool o' water. I says to myself she's stopping somewhere, I says. And I felt it was my duty to go and tell your aunt, whether she was asleep or whether she wasn't asleep.... Well, and there she was, miss, with her eyes closed, and as soft as a child. I spoke to her, loud, more than once. "Miss Carlotta a'n't come," I says. "Miss Carlotta a'n't come, ma'am," I says. She never stirred. Thinks I, this is queer this is. And I goes up to her and touches her. Chilly! Then I takes the liberty of pushing back your poor aunt's eyelids, and I could but see the whites of her eyes; the eyeballs was gone up, and a bit outwards. Yes; and her poor dear chin was dropped. Thinks I, here's trouble, and Miss Carlotta at the concert. I runs to our bedroom, and I tells Lucy to put a cloak on and fetch Dr. Roycroft. "Who for?" she says. "Never you mind who for!" I says, says I. "You up and quick. But you can tell the doctor it's missis as is took." And in ten minutes he was here, miss. But it's only across the garden, like. "Yes," he said, "she's been dead an hour or more. Failure of the heart's action," he said. "She died in her sleep," he said. "Thank God she died in her sleep if she was to die, the pure angel!" I says. I told the doctor as you were away for the night, miss. And I laid her out, miss, and your poor auntie wasn't my first, either. I've seen trouble—I've—'

And Rebecca's tears overcame her voice.

'I'll go upstairs with you, miss,' she struggled out.

One thought that flew across my mind was that Doctor Roycroft was very intimate with the Ryleys, and had doubtless somehow informed them of my aunt's death. This explained Fred Ryley's strange words and attitude to me on the way from the station. The young man had been too timid to stop me. The matter was a trifle, but another idea that struck me was not a trifle, though I strove to make it so. My aunt had died about midnight, and it was at midnight that Diaz and I had heard the mysterious knock on his sitting-room door. At the time I had remarked how it resembled my aunt's knock. Occasionally, when the servants overslept themselves, Aunt Constance would go to their rooms in her pale-blue dressing-gown and knock on their door exactly like that. Could it be that this was one of those psychical manifestations of which I had read? Had my aunt, in passing from this existence to the next, paused a moment to warn me of my terrible danger? My intellect replied that a disembodied soul could not knock, and that the phenomenon had been due simply to some guest or servant of the hotel who had mistaken the room, and discovered his error in time. Nevertheless, the instinctive part of me—that part of us which refuses to fraternize with reason, and which we call the superstitious because we cannot explain it—would not let go the spiritualistic theory, and during all my life has never quite surrendered it to the attacks of my brain.

There was a long pause.

'No,' I said; 'I will go upstairs alone;' and I went, leaving my cloak and hat with Rebecca.

Already, to my hypersensitive nostrils, there was a slight odour in the darkened bedroom. What lay on the bed, straight and long and thin, resembled almost exactly my aunt as she lived. I forced myself to look on it. Except that the face was paler than usual, and had a curious transparent, waxy appearance, and that the cheeks were a little hollowed, and the lines from the nose to the corners of the mouth somewhat deepened, there had been no outward change.... And *this* once was she! I thought, Where is she, then? Where is the soul? Where is that which loved me without understanding me? Where is that which I loved? The baffling, sad enigma of death confronted me in all its terrifying crudity. The shaft of love and the desolation of death had struck me almost in the same hour, and before these twin mysteries, supremely equal, I recoiled and quailed. I had neither faith nor friend. I was solitary, and my soul also was solitary. The difficulties of Being seemed insoluble. I was not a moral coward, I was not prone to facile repentances; but as I gazed at that calm and unsullied mask I realized, whatever I had gained, how much I had lost. At twenty-one I knew more of the fountains of life than Aunt Constance at over sixty. Poor aged thing that had walked among men for interminable years, and never *known*! It seemed impossible, shockingly against Nature, that my aunt's existence should have been so! I pitied her profoundly. I felt that essentially she was girlish compared to me. And yet—and yet—that which she had kept and which I had given away was precious, too—indefinably and wonderfully precious! The price of knowledge and of ecstasy seemed heavy to me then. The girl that had gone with Diaz into that hotel apartment had come out no more. She had expired there, and her extinction was the price, Oh, innocence! Oh, divine ignorance! Oh, refusal! None knows your value save her who has bartered you! And herein is the woman's tragedy.

There in that mausoleum I decided that I must never see Diaz again. He was fast in my heart, a flashing, glorious treasure, but I must never see him again. I must devote myself to memory.

On the dressing-table lay a brown-paper parcel which seemed out of place there. I opened it, and it contained a magnificently-bound copy of *The Imitation of Christ*. Upon the flyleaf was written: 'To dearest Carlotta on attaining her majority. With fondest love. C.P.'

It was too much; it was overwhelming. I wept again. Soul so kind and pure! The sense of my loss, the sense of the simple, proud rectitude of her life, laid me low.

V

Train journeys have too often been sorrowful for me, so much so that the conception itself of a train, crawling over the country like a snake, or flying across it like a winged monster, fills me with melancholy. Trains loaded with human parcels of sadness and illusion and brief joy, wandering about, crossing, and occasionally colliding in the murk of existence; trains warmed and lighted in winter; trains open to catch the air of your own passage in summer; night-trains that pierce the night with your yellow, glaring eyes, and waken mysterious villages, and leave the night behind and run into the dawn as into a station; trains that carry bread and meats for the human parcels, and pillows and fountains of fresh water; trains that sweep haughtily and wearily indifferent through the landscapes and the towns, sufficient unto yourselves, hasty, panting, formidable, and yet mournful entities: I have understood you in your arrogance and your pathos.

That little journey from Knype to Shawport had implanted itself painfully in my memory, as though during it I had peered too close into the face of life. And now I had undertaken another, and a longer one. Three months had elapsed—three months of growing misery and despair; three months of tedious familiarity with lawyers and distant relatives, and all the exasperating camp-followers of death; three months of secret and strange fear, waxing daily. And at last, amid the expostulations and the shrugs of wisdom and age, I had decided to go to London. I had little energy, and no interest, but I saw that I must go to London; I was driven there by my secret fear; I dared not delay. And not a soul in the wide waste of the Five Towns comprehended me, or could have comprehended me had it been so minded. I might have shut up the house for a time. But no; I would not. Always I have been sudden, violent, and arbitrary; I have never been able to tolerate half-measures, or to wait upon occasion. I sold the house; I sold the furniture. Yes; and I dismissed my faithful Rebecca and the clinging Lucy, and they departed, God knows where; it was as though I had sold them into slavery. Again and again, in the final week, I cut myself to the quick, recklessly, perhaps purposely; I moved in a sort of terrible languor, deaf to every appeal, pretending to be stony, and yet tortured by my secret fear, and by a hemorrhage of the heart that no philosophy could stanch. And I swear that nothing desolated me more than the strapping and the labelling of my trunks that morning after I had slept, dreamfully, in the bed that I should never use again—the bed that, indeed, was even then the property of a furniture dealer. Had I wept at all, I should have wept as I wrote out the labels for my trunks: 'Miss Peel, passenger to Golden Cross Hotel, London. Euston via Rugby,' with two thick lines drawn under the 'Euston.' That writing of labels was the climax. With a desperate effort I tore myself up by the roots, and all bleeding I left the Five Towns. I have never seen them since. Some day, when I shall have attained serenity and peace, when the battle has been fought and lost, I will revisit my youth. I have always loved passionately the disfigured hills and valleys of the Five Towns. And as I think of Oldcastle Street, dropping away sleepily and respectably from the Town Hall of Bursley, with the gold angel holding a gold crown on its spire, I vibrate with an inexplicable emotion. What is there in Oldcastle Street to disturb the dust of the soul?

I must tell you here that Diaz had gone to South America on a triumphal tour of concerts, lest I forget! I read it in the paper.

ARNOLD BENNETT

So I arrived in London on a February day, about one o'clock. And the hall-porter at the Golden Cross Hotel, and the two pale girls in the bureau of the hotel, were sympathetic and sweet to me, because I was young and alone, and in mourning, and because I had great rings round my eyes. It was a fine day, blue and mild. At half-past three I had nothing in the world to do. I had come to London without a plan, without a purpose, with scarcely an introduction; I wished simply to plunge myself into its solitude, and to be alone with my secret fear. I walked out into the street, slowly, like one whom ennui has taught to lose no chance of dissipating time. I neither liked nor disliked London. I had no feelings towards it save one of perplexity. I thought it noisy, dirty, and hurried. Its great name roused no thrill in my bosom. On the morrow, I said, I would seek a lodging, and perhaps write to Ethel Ryley. Meanwhile I strolled up into Trafalgar Square, and so into Charing Cross Road. And in Charing Cross Road—it was the curst accident of fate—I saw the signboard of the celebrated old firm of publishers, Oakley and Dalbiac. It is my intention to speak of my books as little as possible in this history. I must, however, explain that six months before my aunt's death I had already written my first novel, *The Jest*, and sent it to precisely Oakley and Dalbiac. It was a wild welter of youthful extravagances, and it aimed to depict London society, of which I knew nothing whatever, with a flippant and cynical pen. Oakley and Dalbiac had kept silence for several months, and had then stated, in an extremely formal epistle, that they thought the book might have some chance of success, and that they would be prepared to publish it on certain terms, but that I must not expect, etc. By that time I had lost my original sublime faith in the exceeding excellence of my story, and I replied that I preferred to withdraw the book. To this letter I had received no answer. When I saw the famous sign over a doorway the impulse seized me to enter and get the manuscript, with the object of rewriting it. Soon, I reflected, I might not be able to enter; the portals of mankind might be barred to me for a space.... I saw in a flash of insight that my salvation lay in work, and in nothing else. I entered, resolutely. A brougham was waiting at the doors.

After passing along counters furnished with ledgers and clerks, through a long, lofty room lined with great pigeon-holes containing thousands of books each wrapped separately in white paper, I was shown into what the clerk who acted as chamberlain called the office of the principal. This room, too, was spacious, but so sombre that the electric light was already burning. The first thing I noticed was that the window gave on a wall of white tiles. In the middle of the somewhat dingy apartment was a vast, square table, and at this table sat a pale, tall man, whose youth astonished me—for the firm of Oakley and Dalbiac was historic.

He did not look up exactly at the instant of my entering, but when he did look up, when he saw me, he stared for an instant, and then sprang from his chair as though magically startled into activity. His age was about thirty, and he had large, dark eyes, and a slight, dark moustache, and his face generally was interesting; he wore a dark gray suit. I was nervous, but he was even more nervous; yet in the moment of looking up he had not seemed nervous. He could not do enough, apparently, to make me feel at ease, and to show his appreciation of me and my work. He spoke enthusiastically of *The Jest*, begging me neither to suppress it nor to alter it. And, without the least suggestion from me, he offered me a considerable sum of money in advance of royalties. At that time I scarcely knew what royalties were. But although my ignorance of business was complete, I guessed that this man was behaving in a manner highly unusual among publishers. He was also patently contradicting the tenor of his firm's letter to me. I thanked him, and said I should like, at any rate, to glance through the manuscript.

'Don't alter it, Miss Peel, I beg,' he said. 'It is "young," I know; but it ought to be. I remember my wife said—my wife reads many of our manuscripts—by the way—' He went to a door, opened it, and called out, 'Mary!'

A tall and slim woman, extremely elegant, appeared in reply to this appeal. Her hair was gray above the ears, and I judged that she was four or five years older than the man. She had a kind, thin face, with shining gray eyes, and she was wearing a hat.

'Mary, this is Miss Peel, the author of *The Jest*—you remember. Miss

Peel, my wife.'

The woman welcomed me with quick, sincere gestures. Her smile was very pleasant, and yet a sad smile. The husband also had an air of quiet, restrained, cheerful sadness.

'My wife is frequently here in the afternoon like this,' said the principal.

'Yes,' she laughed; 'it's quite a family affair, and I'm almost on the staff. I distinctly remember your manuscript, Miss Peel, and how very clever and amusing it was.'

Her praise was spontaneous and cordial, but it was a different thing from the praise of her husband. He obviously noticed the difference.

'I was just saying to Miss Peel—' he began, with increased nervousness.

'Pardon me,' I interrupted. 'But am I speaking to Mr. Oakley or

Mr. Dalbiac?'

'To neither,' said he. 'My name is Ispenlove, and I am the nephew of the late Mr. Dalbiac. Mr. Oakley died thirty years ago. I have no partner.'

'You expected to see a very old gentleman, no doubt,' Mrs. Ispenlove remarked.

'Yes,' I smiled.

'People often do. And Frank is so very young. You live in London?'

'No,' I said; 'I have just come up.'

'To stay?'

'To stay.'

'Alone?'

'Yes. My aunt died a few months ago. I am all that is left of my family.'

Mrs. Ispenlove's eyes filled with tears, and she fingered a gold chain that hung from her neck.

'But have you got rooms—a house?'

'I am at a hotel for the moment.'

'But you have friends?'

I shook my head. Mr. Ispenlove was glancing rapidly from one to the other of us.

'My dear young lady!' exclaimed his wife. Then she hesitated, and said: 'Excuse my abruptness, but do let me beg you to come and have tea with us this afternoon. We live quite near—in Bloomsbury Square. The carriage is waiting. Frank, you can come?'

'I can come for an hour,' said Mr. Ispenlove.

I wanted very much to decline, but I could not. I could not disappoint that honest and generous kindliness, with its touch of melancholy. I could not refuse those shining gray eyes. I saw that my situation and my youth had lacerated Mrs. Ispenlove's sensitive heart, and that she wished to give it balm by being humane to me.

We seemed, so rapid was our passage, to be whisked on an Arabian carpet to a spacious drawing-room, richly furnished, with thick rugs and ample cushions and countless knicknacks and photographs and delicately-tinted lampshades. There was a grand piano by Steinway, and on it Mendelssohn's 'Songs without Words.' The fire slumbered in a curious grate that projected several feet into the room—such a contrivance I had never seen before. Near it sat Mrs. Ispenlove, entrenched behind a vast copper disc on a low wicker stand, pouring out tea. Mr. Ispenlove hovered about. He and his wife called each other 'dearest.' 'Ring the bell for me, dearest.' 'Yes, dearest.' I felt sure that they had no children. They were very intimate, very kind, and always gently sad. The atmosphere was charmingly domestic, even cosy, despite the size of the room—a most pleasing contrast to the offices which we had just left. Mrs. Ispenlove told her husband to look after me well, and he devoted himself to me.

'Do you know,' said Mrs. Ispenlove, 'I am gradually recalling the details of your book, and you are not at all the sort of person that I should have expected to see.'

'But that poor little book isn't *me*,' I answered. 'I shall never write another like it. I only—'

'Shall you not?' Mr. Ispenlove interjected. 'I hope you will, though.'

I smiled.

'I only did it to see what I could do. I am going to begin something quite different.'

'It appears to me,' said Mrs. Ispenlove—'and I must again ask you to excuse my freedom, but I feel as if I had known you a long time—it appears to me that what you want immediately is a complete rest.'

'Why do you say that?' I demanded.

'You do not look well. You look exhausted and worn out.'

I blushed as she gazed at me. Could she—? No. Those simple gray eyes could not imagine evil. Nevertheless, I saw too plainly how foolish I had been. I, with my secret fear, that was becoming less a fear than a dreadful certainty, to permit myself to venture into that house! I might have to fly ignominiously before long, to practise elaborate falsehood, to disappear.

'Perhaps you are right,' I agreed.

The conversation grew fragmentary, and less and less formal. Mrs. Ispenlove was the chief talker. I remember she said that she was always being thrown among clever people, people who could do things, and that her own inability to do anything at all was getting to be an obsession with her; and that people like me could have no idea of the tortures of self-depreciation which she suffered. Her voice was strangely wistful during this confession. She also spoke—once only, and quite shortly, but with what naïve enthusiasm!—of the high mission and influence of the novelist who wrote purely and conscientiously. After this, though my liking for her was undiminished, I had summed her up. Mr. Ispenlove offered no commentary on his wife's sentiments. He struck me as being a reserved man, whose inner life was intense and sufficient to him.

'Ah!' I reflected, as Mrs. Ispenlove, with an almost motherly accent, urged me to have another cup of tea, 'if you knew me, if you knew me, what would you say to me? Would your charity be strong enough to overcome your instincts?' And as I had felt older than my aunt, so I felt older than Mrs. Ispenlove.

I left, but I had to promise to come again on the morrow, after I had seen Mr. Ispenlove on business. The publisher took me down to my hotel in the brougham (and I thought of the drive with Diaz, but the water was not streaming down the windows), and then he returned to his office.

Without troubling to turn on the light in my bedroom, I sank sighing on to the bed. The events of the afternoon had roused me from my terrible lethargy, but now it overcame me again. I tried to think clearly about the Ispenloves and what the new acquaintance meant for me; but I could not think clearly. I had not been able to think clearly for two months. I wished only to die. For a moment I meditated vaguely on suicide, but suicide seemed to involve an amount of complicated enterprise far beyond my capacity. It amazed me how I had managed to reach London. I must have come mechanically, in a heavy dream; for I had no hope, no energy, no vivacity, no interest. For many weeks my mind had revolved round an awful possibility, as if hypnotized by it, and that monotonous revolution seemed alone to constitute my real life. Moreover, I was subject to recurring nausea, and to disconcerting bodily pains and another symptom.

'This must end!' I said, struggling to my feet.

I summoned the courage of an absolute disgust. I felt that the power which had triumphed over my dejection and my irresolution and brought me to London might carry me a little further.

Leaving the hotel, I crossed the Strand. Innumerable omnibuses were crawling past. I jumped into one at hazard, and the conductor put his arm behind my back to support me. He was shouting, 'Putney, Putney, Putney!' in an absent-minded manner: he had assisted me to mount without even looking at me. I climbed to the top of the omnibus and sat down, and the omnibus moved off. I knew not where I was going; Putney was nothing but a name to me.

'Where to, lady?' snapped the conductor, coming upstairs.

'Oh, Putney,' I answered.

A little bell rang and he gave me a ticket. The omnibus was soon full. A woman with a young child shared my seat. But the population of the roof was always changing. I alone remained—so it appeared to me. And we moved interminably forward through the gas-lit and crowded streets, under the mild night. Occasionally, when we came within the circle of an arc-lamp, I could see all my fellow-passengers very clearly; then they were nothing but dark, featureless masses. The horses of the omnibus were changed. A score of times the conductor came briskly upstairs, but he never looked at me again. 'I've done with you,' his back seemed to say.

The houses stood up straight and sinister, thousands of houses unendingly succeeding each other. Some were brilliantly illuminated; some were dark; and some had one or two windows lighted. The phenomenon of a solitary window lighted, high up in a house, filled me with the sense of the tragic romance of London. Why, I cannot tell. But it did. London grew to be almost unbearably mournful. There were too many people in London. Suffering was packed too close. One can contemplate a single affliction with some equanimity, but a million griefs, calamities, frustrations, elbowing each other—No, no! And in all that multitude of sadnesses I felt that mine was the worst. My loneliness, my fear, my foolish youth, my inability to cope with circumstance, my appalling ignorance of the very things which I ought to know! It was awful. And yet even then, in that despairing certainty of disaster, I was conscious of the beauty of life, the beauty of life's exceeding sorrow, and I hugged it to me, like a red-hot iron.

We crossed a great river by a great bridge—a mysterious and mighty stream; and then the streets closed in on us again. And at last, after hours and hours, the omnibus swerved into a dark road and stopped—stopped finally.

'Putney!' cried the conductor, like fate.

I descended. Far off, at the end of the vista of the dark road, I saw a red lamp. I knew that in large cities a red lamp indicated a doctor: it was the one useful thing that I did know.

I approached the red lamp, cautiously, on the other side of the street. Then some power forced me to cross the street and open a wicket. And in the red glow of the lamp I saw an ivory button which I pushed. I could plainly hear the result; it made me tremble. I had a narrow escape of running away. The door was flung wide, and a middle-aged woman appeared in the bright light of the interior of the house. She had a kind face. It is astounding, the number of kind faces one meets.

'Is the doctor in?' I asked.

I would have given a year of my life to hear her say 'No.'

'Yes, miss,' she said. 'Will you step in?'

Events seemed to be moving all too rapidly.

I passed into a narrow hall, with an empty hat-rack, and so into the surgery. From the back of the house came the sound of a piano—scales, played very slowly. The surgery was empty. I noticed a card with letters of the alphabet printed on it in different sizes; and then the piano ceased, and there was the humming of an air in the passage, and a tall man in a frock-coat, slippered and spectacled, came into the surgery.

'Good-evening, madam,' he said gruffly. 'Won't you sit down?'

'I—I—I want to ask you—'

He put a chair for me, and I dropped into it.

'There!' he said, after a moment. 'You felt as if you might faint, didn't you?'

I nodded. The tears came into my eyes.

'I thought so,' he said. 'I'll just give you a draught, if you don't mind.'

He busied himself behind me, and presently I was drinking something out of a conical-shaped glass.

My heart beat furiously, but I felt strong.

'I want you to tell me, doctor,' I spoke firmly, 'whether I am about to become a mother.'

'Ah?' he answered interrogatively, and then he hummed a fragment of an air.

'I have lost my husband,' I was about to add; but suddenly I scorned such a weakness and shut my lips.

'Since when—' the doctor began.

* * * * *

'No,' I heard him saying. 'You have been quite mistaken. But I am not surprised. Such mistakes are frequently made—a kind of auto-suggestion.'

'Mistaken!' I murmured.

I could not prevent the room running round me as I reclined on the sofa; and I fainted.

But in the night, safely in my room again at the hotel, I wondered whether that secret fear, now exorcised, had not also been a hope. I wondered....

PART II

THREE HUMAN HEARTS

I

And now I was twenty-six.

Everyone who knows Jove knows the poignant and delicious day when the lovers, undeclared, but sure of mutual passion, await the magic moment of avowal, with all its changeful consequences. I resume my fragmentary narrative at such a day in my life. As for me, I waited for the avowal as for an earthquake. I felt as though I were the captain of a ship on fire, and the only person aware that the flames were creeping towards a powder magazine. And my love shone fiercely in my heart, like a southern star; it held me, hypnotized, in a thrilling and exquisite entrancement, so that if my secret, silent lover was away from me, as on that fatal night in my drawing-room, my friends were but phantom presences in a shadowy world. This is not an exaggerated figure, but the truth, for when I have loved I have loved much....

My drawing-room in Bedford Court, that night on which the violent drama of my life recommenced, indicated fairly the sorts of success which I had achieved, and the direction of my tastes. The victim of Diaz had gradually passed away, and a new creature had replaced her—a creature rapidly developed, and somewhat brazened in the process under the sun of an extraordinary double prosperity in London. I had soon learnt that my face had a magic to win for me what wealth cannot buy. My books had given me fame and money. And I could not prevent the world from worshipping the woman whom it deemed the gods had greatly favoured. I could not have prevented it, even had I wished, and I did not wish, I knew well that no merit and no virtue, but merely the accident of facial curves, and the accident of a convolution of the brain, had brought me this ascendancy, and at first I reminded myself of the duty of humility. But when homage is reiterated, when the pleasure of obeying a command and satisfying a caprice is begged for, when roses are strewn, and even necks put down in the path, one forgets to be humble; one forgets that in meekness alone lies the sole good; one confuses deserts with the hazards of heredity.

However, in the end fate has no favourites. A woman who has beauty wants to frame it in beauty. The eye is a sensualist, and its appetites, once aroused, grow. A beautiful woman takes the same pleasure in the sight of another beautiful woman as a man does; only jealousy or fear prevents her from admitting the pleasure. I collected beautiful women.... Elegance is a form of beauty. It not only enhances beauty, but it is the one thing which will console the eye for the absence of beauty. The first rule which I made for my home was that in it my eye should not be offended. I lost much, doubtless, by adhering to it, but not more than I gained. And since elegance is impossible without good manners, and good manners are a convention, though a supremely good one, the society by which I surrounded myself was conventional; superficially, of course, for it is the business of a convention to be not more than superficial. Some persons after knowing my drawing-room were astounded by my books, others after reading my books were astounded by my drawing-room; but these persons lacked perception. Given elegance, with or without beauty itself, I had naturally sought, in my friends, intellectual courage, honest thinking, kindness of heart, creative talent, distinction, wit. My search had not been unfortunate.... You see Heaven had been so kind to me!

That night in my drawing-room (far too full of bric-a-brac of all climes and ages), beneath the blaze of the two Empire chandeliers, which Vicary, the musical composer, had found for me in Chartres, there were perhaps a dozen guests assembled.

Vicary had just given, in his driest manner, a description of his recent visit to receive the accolade from the Queen. It was replete with the usual quaint Vicary details—such as the solemn warning whisper of an equerry in Vicary's ear as he walked backwards, *'Mind the edge of the carpet'*; and we all laughed, I absently, and yet a little hysterically—all save Vicary, whose foible was never to laugh. But immediately afterwards there was a pause, one of those disconcerting, involuntary pauses which at a social gathering are like a chill hint of autumn in late summer, and which accuse the hostess. It was over in an instant; the broken current was resumed; everybody pretended that everything was as usual at my receptions. But that pause was the beginning of the downfall.

With a fierce effort I tried to escape from my entrancement, to be interested in these unreal shadows whose voices seemed to come to me from a distance, and to make my glance forget the door, where the one reality in the world for me, my unspoken lover, should have appeared long since. I joined unskilfully in a conversation which Vicary and Mrs. Sardis and her daughter Jocelyn were conducting quite well without my assistance. The rest were chattering now, in one or two groups, except Lord Francis Alcar, who, I suddenly noticed, sat alone on a settee behind the piano. Here was another unfortunate result of my preoccupation. By what negligence had I allowed him to be thus forsaken? I rose and went across to him, penitent, and glad to leave the others.

There are only two fundamental differences in the world—the difference between sex and sex, and the difference between youth and age. Lord Francis Alcar was sixty years older than me. His life was over before mine had commenced. It seemed incredible; but I had acquired the whole of my mundane experience, while he was merely waiting for death. At seventy, men begin to be separated from their fellow-creatures. At eighty, they are like islets sticking out of a sea. At eighty-five, with their trembling and deliberate speech, they are the abstract voice of human wisdom. They gather wisdom with amazing rapidity in the latter years, and even their folly is wise then. Lord Francis was eighty-six; his faculties enfeebled but intact after a career devoted to the three most costly of all luxuries—pretty women, fine pictures, and rare books; a tall, spare man, quietly proud of his age, his ability to go out in the evening unattended, his amorous past, and his contributions to the history of English printing.

As I approached him, he leaned forward into his favourite attitude, elbows on knees and fingertips lightly touching, and he looked up at me. And his eyes, sunken and fatigued and yet audacious, seemed to flash out. He opened his thin lips to speak. When old men speak, they have the air of rousing themselves from an eternal contemplation in order to do so, and what they say becomes accordingly oracular.

'Pallor suits you,' he piped gallantly, and then added: 'But do not carry it to extremes.'

'Am I so pale, then?' I faltered, trying to smile naturally.

I sat down beside him, and smoothed out my black lace dress; he examined it like a connoisseur.

'Yes,' he said at length. 'What is the matter?'

Lord Francis charged this apparently simple and naïve question with a strange intimate meaning. The men who surround a woman such as I, living as I lived, are always demanding, with a secret thirst, 'Does she really live without love? What does she conceal?' I have read this interrogation in the eyes of scores of men; but no one, save Lord Francis, would have had the right to put it into the tones of his voice. We were so mutually foreign and disinterested, so at the opposite ends of life, that he had nothing to gain and I nothing to lose, and I could have permitted to this sage ruin of a male almost a confessor's freedom. Moreover, we had an affectionate regard for each other.

I said nothing, and he repeated in his treble:

'What is the matter?'

'Love is the matter!' I might have passionately cried out to him, had we been alone. But I merely responded to his tone with my eyes. I thanked him with my eyes for his bold and flattering curiosity, senile, but thoroughly masculine to the last. And I said:

'I am only a little exhausted. I finished my novel yesterday.'

It was my sixth novel in five years.

'With you,' he said, 'work is simply a drug.'

'Lord Francis,' I expostulated, 'how do you know that?'

'And it has got such a hold of you that you cannot do without it,' he proceeded, with slow, faint shrillness. 'Some women take to morphia, others take to work.'

'On the contrary,' I said, 'I have quite determined to do no more work for twelve months.'

'Seriously?'

'Seriously.'

He faced me, vivacious, and leaned against the back of the settee.

'Then you mean to give yourself time to love?' he murmured, as it were with a kind malice, and every crease in his veined and yellow features was intensified by an enigmatic smile.

'Why not?' I laughed encouragingly. 'Why not? What do you advise?'

'I advise it,' he said positively. 'I advise it. You have already wasted the best years.'

'The best?'

'One can never afterwards love as one loves at twenty. But there! You have nothing to learn about love!'

He gave me one of those disrobing glances of which men who have dedicated their existence to women alone have the secret. I shrank under the ordeal; I tried to clutch my clothes about me.

The chatter from the other end of the room grew louder. Vicary was gazing critically at his chandeliers.

'Does love bring happiness?' I asked Lord Francis, carefully ignoring his remark.

'For forty years,' he quavered, 'I made love to every pretty woman I met, in the search for happiness. I may have got five per cent. return on my outlay, which is perhaps not bad in these hard times; but I certainly did not get even that in happiness. I got it in—other ways.'

'And if you had to begin afresh?'

He stood up, turned his back on the room, and looked down at me from his bent height. His knotted hands were shaking, as they always shook.

'I would do the same again,' he whispered.

'Would you?' I said, looking up at him. 'Truly?'

'Yes. Only the fool and the very young expect happiness. The wise merely hope to be interested, at least not to be bored, in their passage through this world. Nothing is so interesting as love and grief, and the one involves the other. Ah! would I not do the same again!'

He spoke gravely, wistfully, and vehemently, as if employing the last spark of divine fire that was left in his decrepit frame. This undaunted confession of a faith which had survived twenty years of inactive meditation, this banner waved by an expiring arm in the face of the eternity that mocks at the transience of human things, filled me with admiration. My eyes moistened, but I continued to look up at him.

'What is the title of the new book?' he demanded casually, sinking into a chair.

'*Burning Sappho*,' I answered. 'But the title is very misleading.'

'Bright star!' he exclaimed, taking my hand. 'With such a title you will surely beat the record of the Good Dame.'

'Hsh!' I enjoined him.

Jocelyn Sardis was coming towards us.

The Good Dame was the sobriquet which Lord Francis had invented to conceal—or to display—his courteous disdain of the ideals represented by Mrs. Sardis, that pillar long established, that stately dowager, that impeccable *doyenne* of serious English fiction. Mrs. Sardis had captured two continents. Her novels, dealing with all the profound problems of the age, were read by philosophers and politicians, and one of them had reached a circulation of a quarter of a million copies. Her dignified and indefatigable pen furnished her with an income of fifteen thousand pounds a year.

Jocelyn Sardis was just entering her mother's world, and she had apparently not yet recovered from the surprise of the discovery that she was a woman; a simple and lovable young creature with brains amply sufficient for the making of apple-pies. As she greeted Lord Francis in her clear, innocent voice, I wondered sadly why her mother should be so anxious to embroider the work of Nature. I thought if Jocelyn could just be left alone to fall in love with some average, kindly stockbroker, how much more nearly the eternal purpose might be fulfilled....

'Yes, I remember,' Lord Francis was saying. 'It was at St. Malo. And what did you think of the Breton peasant?'

'Oh,' said Jocelyn, 'mamma has not yet allowed us to study the condition of the lower classes in France. We are all so busy with the new Settlement.'

'It must be very exhausting, my dear child,' said Lord Francis.

I rose.

'I came to ask you to play something,' the child appealed to me. 'I have never heard you play, and everyone says—'

'Jocelyn, my pet,' the precise, prim utterance of Mrs. Sardis floated across the room.

'What, mamma?'

'You are not to trouble Miss Peel. Perhaps she does not feel equal to playing.'

My blood rose in an instant. I cannot tell why, unless it was that I resented from Mrs. Sardis even the slightest allusion to the fact that I was not entirely myself. The latent antagonism between us became violently active in my heart. I believe I blushed. I know that I felt murderous towards Mrs. Sardis. I gave her my most adorable smile, and I said, with sugar in my voice:

'But I shall be delighted to play for Jocelyn.'

It was an act of bravado on my part to attempt to play the piano in the mood in which I found myself; and that I should have begun the opening phrase of Chopin's first Ballade, that composition so laden with formidable memories—begun it without thinking and without apprehension—showed how far I had lost my self-control. Not that the silver sounds which shimmered from the Broadwood under my feverish hands filled me with sentimental regrets for an irrecoverable past. No! But I saw the victim of Diaz as though I had never been she. She was for me one of those ladies that have loved and are dead. The simplicity of her mind and her situation, compared with my mind and my situation, seemed unbearably piteous to me. Why, I knew not. The pathos of that brief and vanished idyll overcame me like some sad story of an antique princess. And then, magically, I saw the pathos of my present position in it as in a truth-revealing mirror. My fame, and my knowledge and my experience, my trained imagination, my skill, my social splendour, my wealth, were stripped away from me as inessential, and I was merely a woman in love, to whom love could not fail to bring calamity and grief; a woman expecting her lover, and yet to whom his coming could only be disastrous; a woman with a heart divided between tremulous joy and dull sorrow; who was at once in heaven and in hell; the victim of love. How often have I called my dead Carlotta the victim of Diaz! Let me be less unjust, and say that he, too, was the victim of love. What was Diaz but the instrument of the god?

Jocelyn stood near me by the piano. I glanced at her as I played, and smiled. She answered my smile; her eyes glistened with tears; I bent my gaze suddenly to the keyboard. 'You too!' I thought sadly, 'You too!... One day! One day even you will know what life is, and the look in those innocent eyes will never be innocent again!'

Then there was a sharp crack at the other end of the room; the handle of the door turned, and the door began to open. My heart bounded and stopped. It must be he, at last! I perceived the fearful intensity of my longing for his presence. But it was only a servant with a tray. My fingers stammered and stumbled. For a few instants I forced them to obey me;

my pride was equal to the strain, though I felt sick and fainting. And then I became aware that my guests were staring at me with alarmed and anxious faces. Mrs. Sardis had started from her chair. I dropped my hands. It was useless to fight further; the battle was lost.

'I will not play any more,' I said quickly. 'I ought not to have tried to play from memory. Excuse me.'

And I left the piano as calmly as I could. I knew that by an effort I could walk steadily and in a straight line across the room to Vicary and the others, and I succeeded. They should not learn my secret.

'Poor thing!' murmured Mrs. Sardis sympathetically. 'Do sit down, dear.'

'Won't you have something to drink?' said Vicary.

'I am perfectly all right,' I said. 'I'm only sorry that my memory is not what it used to be.' And I persisted in standing for a few moments by the mantelpiece. In the glass I caught one glimpse of a face as white as milk, Jocelyn remained at her post by the piano, frightened by she knew not what, like a young child.

'Our friend finished a new work only yesterday,' said Lord Francis shakily. He had followed me. 'She has wisely decided to take a long holiday. Good-bye, my dear.'

These were the last words he ever spoke to me, though I saw him again. We shook hands in silence, and he left. Nor would the others stay. I had ruined the night. We were all self-conscious, diffident, suspicious. Even Vicary was affected. How thankful I was that my silent lover had not come! My secret was my own—and his. And no one should surprise it unless we chose. I cared nothing what they thought, or what they guessed, as they filed out of the door, a brilliant procession of which I had the right to be proud; they could not guess my secret. I was sufficiently woman of the world to baffle them as long as I wished to baffle them.

Then I noticed that Mrs. Sardis had stayed behind; she was examining some lustre ware in the further drawing-room.

'I'm afraid Jocelyn has gone without her mother,' I said, approaching her.

'I have told Jocelyn to go home alone,' replied Mrs. Sardis. 'The carriage will return for me. Dear friend, I want to have a little talk with you. Do you permit?'

'I shall be delighted,' I said.

'You are sure you are well enough?'

'There is nothing whatever the matter with me,' I answered slowly and distinctly. 'Come to the fire, and let us be comfortable. And I told Emmeline Palmer, my companion and secretary, who just then appeared, that she might retire to bed.

Mrs. Sardis was nervous, and this condition, so singular in Mrs. Sardis, naturally made me curious as to the cause of it. But my eyes still furtively wandered to the door.

'My dear co-worker,' she began, and hesitated.

'Yes,' I encouraged her.

She put her matron's lips together:

'You know how proud I am of your calling, and how jealous I am of its honour and its good name, and what a great mission I think we novelists have in the work of regenerating the world.'

I nodded. That kind of eloquence always makes me mute. It leaves nothing to be said.

'I wonder,' Mrs. Sardis continued, 'if you have ever realized what a power *you* are in England and America to-day.'

'Power!' I echoed. 'I have done nothing but try to write as honestly and as well as I could what I felt I wanted to write.'

'No one can doubt your sincerity, my dear friend,' Mrs. Sardis said. 'And I needn't tell you that I am a warm admirer of your talent, and that I rejoice in your success. But the tendency of your work—'

'Surely,' I interrupted her coldly, 'you are not taking the trouble to tell me that my books are doing harm to the great and righteous Anglo-Saxon public!'

'Do not let us poke fun at our public, my dear,' she protested. 'I personally do not believe that your books are harmful, though their originality is certainly daring, and their realism startling; but there exists a considerable body of opinion, as you know, that strongly objects to your books. It may be reactionary opinion, bigoted opinion, ignorant opinion, what you like, but it exists, and it is not afraid to employ the word "immoral."'

'What, then?'

'I speak as one old enough to be your mother, and I speak after all to a motherless young girl who happens to have genius with, perhaps, some of the disadvantages of genius, when I urge you so to arrange your personal life that this body of quite respectable adverse opinion shall not find in it a handle to use against the fair fame of our calling.'

'Mrs. Sardis!' I cried. 'What do you mean?'

I felt my nostrils dilate in anger as I gazed, astounded, at this incarnation of mediocrity who had dared to affront me on my own hearth; and by virtue of my youth and my beauty, and all the homage I had received, and the clear sincerity of my vision of life, I despised and detested the mother of a family who had never taken one step beyond the conventions in which she was born. Had she not even the wit to perceive that I was accustomed to be addressed as queens are addressed?... Then, as suddenly as it had flamed, my anger cooled, for I could see the painful earnestness in her face. And Mrs. Sardis and I—what were we but two groups of vital instincts, groping our respective ways out of one mystery into another? Had we made ourselves? Had we chosen our characters? Mrs. Sardis was fulfilling herself, as I was. She was a natural force, as I was. As well be angry with a hurricane, or the heat of the sun.

'What do you mean?' I repeated quietly. 'Tell me exactly what you mean.'

I thought she was aiming at the company which I sometimes kept, or the freedom of my diversions on the English Sabbath. I thought what trifles were these compared to the dilemma in which, possibly within a few hours, I should find myself.

'To put it in as few words as possible,' said she, 'I mean your relations with a married man. Forgive my bluntness, dear girl.'

'My—'

Then my secret was not my secret! We were chattered about, he and I. We had not hidden our feeling, our passions. And I had been imagining myself a woman of the world equal to sustaining a difficult part in the masque of existence. With an abandoned gesture I hid my face in my hands for a moment, and then I dropped my hands, and leaned forward and looked steadily at Mrs. Sardis. Her eyes were kind enough.

'You won't affect not to understand?' she said.

I assented with a motion of the head.

'Many persons say there is a—a liaison between you,' she said.

'And do you think that?' I asked quickly.

'If I had thought so, my daughter would not have been here to-night,' she said solemnly. 'No, no; I do not believe it for an instant, and I brought Jocelyn specially to prove to the world that I do not. I only heard the gossip a few days ago; and to-night, as I sat here, it was borne in upon me that I must speak to you to-night. And I have done so. Not everyone would have done so, dear girl. Most of your friends are content to talk among themselves.'

'About me? Oh!' It was the expression of an almost physical pain.

'What can you expect them to do?' asked Mrs. Sardis mildly.

'True,' I agreed.

'You see, the circumstances are so extremely peculiar. Your friendship with her—'

'Let me tell you'—I stopped her—'that not a single word has ever passed between me and—and the man you mean, that everybody might not hear. Not a single word!'

'Dearest girl,' she exclaimed; 'how glad I am! How glad I am! Now I can take measures to—.

'But—' I resumed.

'But what?'

In a flash I saw the futility of attempting to explain to a woman like Mrs. Sardis, who had no doubts about the utter righteousness of her own code, whose rules had no exceptions, whose principles could apply to every conceivable case, and who was the very embodiment of the vast stolid London that hemmed me in—of attempting to explain to such an excellent, blind creature why, and in obedience to what ideal, I would not answer for the future. I knew that I might as well talk to a church steeple.

'Nothing,' I said, rising, 'except that I thank you. Be sure that I am grateful. You have had a task which must have been very unpleasant to you.'

She smiled, virtuously happy.

'You made it easy,' she murmured.

I perceived that she wanted to kiss me; but I avoided the caress. How I hated kissing women!

'No more need be said,' she almost whispered, as I put my hand on the knob of the front-door. I had escorted her myself to the hall.

'Only remember your great mission, the influence you wield, and the fair fame of our calling.'

My impulse was to shriek. But I merely smiled as decently as I could; and

I opened the door.

And there, on the landing, just emerging from the lift, was Ispenlove, haggard, pale, his necktie astray. He and Mrs. Sardis exchanged a brief stare; she gave me a look of profound pain and passed in dignified silence down the stairs; Ispenlove came into the flat.

'Nothing will convince her now that I am not a liar,' I reflected.

It was my last thought as I sank, exquisitely drowning, in the sea of sensations caused by Ispenlove's presence.

II

Without a word, we passed together into the drawing-room, and I closed the door. Ispenlove stood leaning against the piano, as though intensely fatigued; he crushed his gibus with an almost savage movement, and then bent his large, lustrous black eyes absently on the flat top of it. His thin face was whiter even than usual, and his black hair, beard, and moustache all dishevelled; the collar of his overcoat was twisted, and his dinner-jacket rose an inch above it at the back of the neck.

I wanted to greet him, but I could not trust my lips. And I saw that he, too, was trying in vain to speak.

At length I said, with that banality which too often surprises us in supreme moments:

'What is it? Do you know that your tie is under your ear?'

And as I uttered these words, my voice, breaking of itself and in defiance of me, descended into a tone which sounded harsh and inimical.

'Ah!' he murmured, lifting his eyes to mine, 'if you turn against me to-night, I shall—'

'Turn against you!' I cried, shocked. 'Let me help you with your overcoat!'

And I went near him, meaning to take his overcoat.

'It's finished between Mary and me,' he said, holding me with his gaze.

'It's finished. I've no one but you now; and I've come—I've come—'

He stopped. We read one another's eyes at arm's length, and all the sorrow and pity and love that were in each of us rose to our eyes and shone there. I shivered with pleasure when I saw his arms move, and then he clutched and dragged me to him, and I hid my glowing face on his shoulder, in the dear folds of his overcoat, and I felt his lips on my neck. And then, since neither of us was a coward, we lifted our heads, and our mouths met honestly and fairly, and, so united, we shut our eyes for an eternal moment, and the world was not.

Such was the avowal.

I gave up my soul to him in that long kiss; all that was me, all that was most secret and precious in me, ascended and poured itself out through my tense lips, and was received by him. I kissed him with myself, with the entire passionate energy of my being—not merely with my mouth. And if I sighed, it was because I tried to give him more—more than I had—and failed. Ah! The sensation of his nearness, the warmth of his face, the titillation of his hair, the slow, luxurious intake of our breaths, the sweet cruelty of his desperate clutch on my shoulders, the glimpses of his skin through my eyelashes when I raised ever so little my eyelids! Pain and joy of life, you were mingled then!

I remembered that I was a woman, and disengaged myself and withdrew from him. I hated to do it; but I did it. We became self-conscious. The brilliant and empty drawing-room scanned us unfavourably with all its globes and mirrors. How difficult it is to be natural in a great crisis! Our spirits clamoured for expression, beating vainly against a thousand barred doors of speech. There was so much to say, to explain, to define, and everything was so confused and dizzily revolving, that we knew not which door to open first. And then I think we both felt, but I more than he, that explanations and statements were futile, that even if all the doors were thrown open together, they would be inadequate. The deliciousness of silence, of wonder, of timidity, of things guessed at and hidden....

'It makes me afraid,' he murmured at length.

'What?'

'To be loved like that.... Your kiss ... you don't know.'

I smiled almost sadly. As if I did not know what my kiss had done! As if I did not know that my kiss had created between us the happiness which brings ruin!

'You *do* love me?' he demanded.

I nodded, and sat down.

'Say it, say it!' he pleaded.

'More than I can ever show you,' I said proudly.

'Honestly,' he said, 'I can't imagine what you have been able to see in me. I'm nothing—I'm nobody—'

'Foolish boy!' I exclaimed. 'You are you.'

The profound significance of that age-worn phrase struck me for the first time.

He rushed to me at the word 'boy,' and, standing over me, took my hand in his hot hand. I let it lie, inert.

'But you haven't always loved me. I have always loved *you,* from the moment when I drove with you, that first day, from the office to your hotel. But you haven't always loved me.'

'No,' I admitted.

'Then when did you—? Tell me.'

'I was dull at first—I could not see. But when you told me that the end of *Fate and Friendship* was not as good as I could make it—do you remember, that afternoon in the office?—and how reluctant you were to tell me, how afraid you were to tell me?—your throat went dry, and you stroked your forehead as you always do when you are nervous—There! you are doing it now, foolish boy!'

I seized his left arm, and gently pulled it down from his face. Oh, exquisite moment!

'It was brave of you to tell me—very brave! I loved you for telling me. You were quite wrong about the end of that book. You didn't see the fine point of it, and you never would have seen it—and I liked you, somehow, for not seeing it, because it was so feminine—but I altered the book to please you, and when I had altered it, against my conscience, I loved you more.'

'It's incredible! incredible!' he muttered, half to himself. 'I never hoped till lately that you would care for me. I never dared to think of such a thing. I knew you oughtn't to! It passes comprehension.'

'That is just what love does,' I said.

'No, no,' he went on quickly; 'you don't understand; you can't understand my feelings when I began to suspect, about two months ago, that, after all, the incredible had happened. I'm nothing but your publisher. I can't talk. I can't write. I can't play. I can't do anything. And look at the men you have here! I've sometimes wondered how often you've been besieged—'

'None of them was like you,' I said. 'Perhaps that is why I have always kept them off.'

I raised my eyes and lips, and he stooped and kissed me. He wanted to take me in his arms again, but I would not yield myself.

'Be reasonable,' I urged him. 'Ought we not to think of our situation?'

He loosed me, stammering apologies, abasing himself.

'I ought to leave you, I ought never to see you again.' He spoke roughly.

'What am I doing to you? You who are so innocent and pure!'

'I entreat you not to talk like that,' I gasped, reddening.

'But I must talk like that,' he insisted. 'I must talk like that. You had everything that a woman can desire, and I come into your life and offer you—what?'

'I *have* everything a woman can desire,' I corrected him softly.

'Angel!' he breathed. 'If I bring you disaster, you will forgive me, won't you?'

'My happiness will only cease with your love,' I said.

'Happiness!' he repeated. 'I have never been so happy as I am now; but such happiness is terrible. It seems to me impossible that such happiness can last.'

'Faint heart!' I chided him.

'It is for you I tremble,' he said. 'If—if—' He stopped. 'My darling, forgive me!'

How I pitied him! How I enveloped him in an effluent sympathy that rushed warm from my heart! He accused himself of having disturbed my existence. Whereas, was it not I who had disturbed his? He had fought against me, I knew well, but fate had ordained his defeat. He had been swept away; he had been captured; he had been caught in a snare of the high gods. And he was begging forgiveness, he who alone had made my life worth living! I wanted to kneel before him, to worship him, to dry his tears with my hair. I swear that my feelings were as much those of a mother as of a lover. He was ten years older than me, and yet he seemed boyish, and I an aged woman full of experience, as he sat there opposite to me with his wide, melancholy eyes and restless mouth.

'Wonderful, is it not,' he said, 'that we should be talking like this to-night, and only yesterday we were Mr. and Miss to each other?'

'Wonderful!' I responded. 'But yesterday we talked with our eyes, and our eyes did not say Mr. or Miss. Our eyes said—Ah, what they said can never be translated into words!'

My gaze brooded on him like a caress, explored him with the unappeasable curiosity of love, and blinded him like the sun. Could it be true that Heaven had made that fine creature—noble and modest, nervous and full of courage, impetuous and self-controlled, but, above all things, fine and delicate—could it be true that Heaven had made him and then given him to me, with his enchanting imperfections that themselves constituted perfection? Oh, wonder, wonder! Oh, miraculous bounty which I had not deserved! This thing had happened to me, of all women! How it showed, by comparison, the sterility of my success and my fame and my worldly splendour! I had hungered and thirsted for years; I had travelled interminably through the hot desert of my brilliant career, until I had almost ceased to hope that I should reach, one evening, the pool of water and the palm. And now I might eat and drink and rest in the shade. Wonderful!

'Why were you so late to-night?' I asked abruptly.

'Late?' he replied absently. 'Is it late?'

We both looked at the clock. It was yet half an hour from midnight.

'Of course it isn't—not *very*,' I said. I was forgetting that.

Everybody left so early.'

'Why was that?'

I told him, in a confusion that was sweet to me, how I had suffered by reason of his failure to appear. He glanced at me with tender amaze.

'But I am fortunate to-day,' I exclaimed. 'Was it not lucky they left when they did? Suppose you had arrived, in that state, dearest man, and burst into a room full of people? What would they have thought? Where should I have looked?'

'Angel!' he cried. 'I'm so sorry. I forgot it was your evening. I must have forgotten. I forgot everything, except that I was bound to see you at once, instantly, with all speed.'

Poor boy! He was like a bird fluttering in my hand. Millions of women must have so pictured to themselves the men who loved them, and whom they loved.

'But still, you *were* rather late, you know,' I smiled.

'Do not ask me why,' he begged, with an expression of deep pain on his face. 'I have had a scene with Mary. It would humiliate me to tell you—to tell even you—what passed between us. But it is over. Our relations in the future can never, in any case, be more than formal.'

A spasm of fierce jealousy shot through me—jealousy of Mary, my friend Mary, who knew him with such profound intimacy that they could go through a scene together which was 'humiliating.' I saw that my own intimacy with him was still crude with the crudity of newness, and that only years could mellow it. Mary, the good, sentimental Mary, had wasted the years of their marriage—had never understood the value of the treasure in her keeping. Why had they always been sad in their house? What was the origin of that resigned and even cheerful gloom which had pervaded their domestic life, and which I had remarked on my first visit to Bloomsbury Square? Were these, too, mysteries that I must not ask my lover to reveal? Resentment filled me. I came near to hating Mary, not because she had made him unhappy—oh no!—but because she had had the priority in his regard, and because there was nothing about him, however secret and recondite, that I could be absolutely sure of the sole knowledge of. She had been in the depths with him. I desired fervently that I also might descend with him, and even deeper. Oh, that I might have the joy and privilege of humiliation with him!

'I shall ask you nothing, dearest,' I murmured.

I had risen from my seat and gone to him, and was lightly touching his hair with my fingers. He did not move, but sat staring into the fire. Somehow, I adored him because he made no response to the fondling of my hand. His strange acceptance of the caress as a matter of course gave me the illusion that I was his wife, and that the years had mellowed our intimacy.

'Carlotta!'

He spoke my name slowly and distinctly, savouring it.

'Yes,' I answered softly and obediently.

'Carlotta! Listen! Our two lives are in our hands at this moment—this moment while we talk here.'

His rapt eyes had not stirred from the fire.

'I feel it,' I said.

'What are we to do? What shall we decide to do?'

He slowly turned towards me. I lowered my glance.

'I don't know,' I said.

'Yes, you do, Carlotta,' he insisted. 'You do know.'

His voice trembled.

'Mary and I are such good friends,' I said. 'That is what makes it so—'

'No, no, no!' he objected loudly. His nervousness had suddenly increased. 'Don't, for God's sake, begin to argue in that way! You are above feminine logic. Mary is your friend. Good. You respect her; she respects you. Good.

Is that any reason why our lives should be ruined? Will that benefit Mary? Do I not tell you that everything has ceased between us?'

'The idea of being false to Mary—'

'There's no question of being false. And if there was, would you be false to love rather than to friendship? Between you and me there is love; between Mary and me there is not love. It isn't her fault, nor mine, least of all yours. It is the fault of the secret essence of existence. Have you not yourself written that the only sacred thing is instinct? Are we, or are we not, to be true to ourselves?'

'You see,' I said, 'your wife is so sentimental. She would be incapable of looking at the affair as—as we do; as I should in her place.'

I knew that my protests were insincere, and that all my heart and brain were with him, but I could not admit this frankly. Ah! And I knew also that the sole avenue to peace and serenity, not to happiness, was the path of renunciation and of obedience to the conventions of society, and that this was precisely the path which we should never take. And on the horizon of our joy I saw a dark cloud. It had always been there, but I had refused to see it. I looked at it now steadily.

'Of course,' he groaned, 'if we are to be governed by Mary's sentimentality—'

'Dear love,' I whispered, 'what do you want me to do?'

'The only possible, honest, just thing. I want you to go away with me, so that Mary can get a divorce.'

He spoke sternly, as it were relentlessly.

'Does she guess—about me?' I asked, biting my lip, and looking away from him.

'Not yet. Hasn't the slightest notion, I'm sure. But I'll tell her, straight and fair.'

'Dearest friend,' I said, after a silence. 'Perhaps I know more of the world than you think. Perhaps I'm a girl only in years and situation. Forgive me if I speak plainly. Mary may prove unfaithfulness, but she cannot get a decree unless she can prove other things as well.'

He stroked his forehead. As for me, I shuddered with agitation. He walked across the room and back.

'Angel!' he said, putting his white face close to mine like an actor. 'I will prove whether your love for me is great enough. I have struck her. I struck her to-night in the presence of a servant. And I did it purposely, in cold blood, so that she might be able to prove cruelty. Ah! Have I not thought it all out? Have I not?'

A sob, painfully escaping, shook my whole frame.

'And this was before you had—had spoken to me!' I said bitterly.

Not myself, but some strange and frigid force within me uttered those words.

'That is what love will do. That is the sort of thing love drives one to,' he cried despairingly. 'Oh! I was not sure of you—I was not sure of you. I struck her, on the off chance.'

And he sank on the sofa and wept passionately, unashamed, like a child.

I could not bear it. My heart would have broken if I had watched, without assuaging, my boy's grief an instant longer than I did. I sprang to him. I took him to my breast. I kissed his eyes until the tears ceased to flow. Whatever it was or might be, I must share his dishonour.

'My poor girl!' he said at length. 'If you had refused me, if you had even judged me, I intended to warn you plainly that it meant my death; and if that failed, I should have gone to the office and shot myself.'

'Do not say such things,' I entreated him.

'But it is true. The revolver is in my pocket. Ah! I have made you cry!

You're frightened! But I'm not a brute; I'm only a little beside myself.

Pardon me, angel!'

He kissed me, smiling sadly with a trace of humour. He did not understand me. He did not suspect the risk he had run. If I had hesitated to surrender, and he had sought to move me by threatening suicide, I should never have surrendered. I knew myself well enough to know that. I had a conscience that was incapable of yielding to panic. A threat would have parted us, perhaps for ever. Oh, the blindness of man! But I forgave him. Nay, I cherished him the more for his childlike, savage simplicity.

'Carlotta,' he said, 'we shall leave everything. You grasp it?—everything.'

'Yes,' I replied. 'Of all the things we have now, we shall have nothing but ourselves.'

'If I thought it was a sacrifice for you, I would go out and never see you again.'

Noble fellow, proud now in the certainty that he sufficed for me! He meant what he said.

'It is no sacrifice for me,' I murmured. 'The sacrifice would be not to give up all in exchange for you.'

'We shall be exiles,' he went on, 'until the divorce business is over. And then perhaps we shall creep back—shall we?—and try to find out how many of our friends are our equals in moral courage.'

'Yes,' I said. 'We shall come back. They all do.'

'What do you mean?' he demanded.

'Thousands have done what we are going to do,' I said. 'And all of them have thought that their own case was different from the other cases.'

'Ah!'

'And a few have been happy. A few have not regretted the price. A few have retained the illusion.'

'Illusion? Dearest girl, why do you talk like this?'

I could see that my heart's treasure was ruffled. He clasped my hand tenaciously.

'I must not hide from you the kind of woman you have chosen,' I answered quietly, and as I spoke a hush fell upon my amorous passion. 'In me there are two beings—myself and the observer of myself. It is the novelist's disease, this duplication of personality. When I said illusion, I meant the supreme illusion of love. Is it not an illusion? I have seen it in others, and in exactly the same way I see it in myself and I see it in you. Will it last?—who knows? None can tell.'

'Angel!' he expostulated.

'No one can foresee the end of love,' I said, with an exquisite gentle sorrow. 'But when the illusion is as intense as mine, as yours, even if its hour is brief, that hour is worth all the terrible years of disillusion which it will cost. Darling, this precious night alone would not be too dear if I paid for it with the rest of my life.'

He thanked me with a marvellous smile of confident adoration, and his disengaged hand played with the gold chain which hung loosely round my neck.

'Call it illusion if you like,' he said. 'Words are nothing. I only know that for me it will be eternal. I only know that my one desire is to be with you always, never to leave you, not to miss a moment of you; to have you for mine, openly, securely. Carlotta, where shall we go?'

'We must travel, mustn't we?'

'Travel?' he repeated, with an air of discontent. 'Yes. But where to?'

'Travel,' I said. 'See things. See the world.'

'I had thought we might find some quiet little place,' he said wistfully, and as if apologetically, where we could be alone, undisturbed, some spot where we could have ourselves wholly to ourselves, and go walks into mountains and return for dinner; and then the long, calm evenings! Dearest, our honeymoon!'

Our honeymoon! I had not, in the pursuit of my calling, studied human nature and collected documents for nothing. With how many brides had I not talked! How many loves did I not know to have been paralyzed and killed by a surfeit in the frail early stages of their existence! Inexperienced as I was, my learning in humanity was wiser than the experience of my impulsive, generous, magnanimous lover, to whom the very thought of calculation would have been abhorrent. But I saw, I felt, I lived through in a few seconds the interminable and monotonous length of those calm days, and especially those calm evenings succeeding each other with a formidable sameness. I had watched great loves faint and die. And I knew that our love—miraculously sweet as it was—probably was not greater than many great ones that had not stood the test. You perceive the cold observer in me. I knew that when love lasted, the credit of the survival was due far more often to the woman than to the man. The woman must husband herself, dole herself out, economize herself so that she might be splendidly wasteful when need was. The woman must plan, scheme, devise, invent, reconnoitre, take precautions; and do all this sincerely and lovingly in the name and honour of love. A passion, for her, is a campaign; and her deadliest enemy is satiety. Looking into my own heart, and into his, I saw nothing but hope for the future of our love. But the beautiful plant must not be exposed to hazard. Suppose it sickened, such a love as ours—what then? The misery of hell, the torture of the damned! Only its rich and ample continuance could justify us.

'My dear,' I said submissively, 'I shall leave everything to you. The idea of travelling occurred to me; that was all. I have never travelled further than Cannes. Still, we have all our lives before us.'

'We will travel,' he said unselfishly. 'We'll go round the world—slowly. I'll get the tickets at Cook's to-morrow.'

'But, dearest, if you would rather—'

'No, no! In any case we shall always have our evenings.'

'Of course we shall. Dearest, how good you are!'

'I wish I was,' he murmured.

I was glad, then, that I had never allowed my portrait to appear in a periodical. We could not prevent the appearance in American newspapers of heralding paragraphs, but the likelihood of our being recognised was sensibly lessened.

'Can you start soon?' he asked. 'Can you be ready?'

'Any time. The sooner the better, now that it is decided.'

'You do not regret? We have decided so quickly. Ah! you are the merest girl, and I have taken advantage—'

I put my hand over his mouth. He seized it, and kept it there and kissed it, and his ardent breath ran through my fingers.

'What about your business?' I said.

'I shall confide it to old Tate—tell him some story—he knows quite as much about it as I do. To-morrow I will see to all that. The day after, shall we start? No; to-morrow night. To-morrow night, eh? I'll run in to-morrow and tell you what I've arranged. I must see you to-morrow, early.'

'No,' I said. 'Do not come before lunch.'

'Not before lunch! Why?'

He was surprised. But I had been my own mistress for five years, with my own habits, rules, privacies. I had never seen anyone before lunch. And to-morrow, of all days, I should have so much to do and to arrange. Was this man to come like an invader and disturb my morning? So felt the celibate in me, instinctively, thoughtlessly. That deep-seated objection to the intrusion of even the most loved male at certain times is common, I think, to all women. Women are capable of putting love aside, like a rich dress, and donning the *peignoir* of matter-of-fact dailiness, in a way which is an eternal enigma to men.... Then I saw, in a sudden flash, that I had renounced my individual existence, that I had forfeited my habits and rules, and privacies, that I was a man's woman. And the passionate lover in me gloried in this.

'Come as soon as you like, dearest friend,' I said.

'Nobody except Mary will know anything till we are actually gone,' he remarked. 'And I shall not tell her till the last thing. Afterwards, won't they chatter! God! Let 'em.'

'They are already chattering,' I said. And I told him about Mrs. Sardis. 'When she met you on the landing,' I added, 'she drew her own conclusions, my poor, poor boy!'

He was furious. I could see he wanted to take me in his arms and protect me masculinely from the rising storm.

'All that is nothing,' I soothed him. 'Nothing. Against it, we have our self-respect. We can scorn all that.' And I gave a short, contemptuous laugh.

'Darling!' he murmured. 'You are more than a woman.'

'I hope not.' And I laughed again, but unnaturally.

He had risen; I leaned back in a large cushioned chair; we looked at each other in silence—a silence that throbbed with the heavy pulse of an unutterable and complex emotion—pleasure, pain, apprehension, even terror. What had I done? Why had I, with a word—nay, without a word, with merely a gesture and a glance—thrown my whole life into the crucible of passion? Why did I exult in the tremendous and impetuous act, like a martyr, and also like a girl? Was I playing with my existence as an infant plays with a precious bibelot that a careless touch may shatter? Why was I so fiercely, madly, drunkenly happy when I gazed into those eyes?

'I suppose I must go,' he said disconsolately.

I nodded, and the next instant the clock struck.

'Yes,' he urged himself, 'I must go.'

He bent down, put his hands on the arms of the chair, and kissed me violently, twice. The fire that consumes the world ran scorchingly through me. Every muscle was suddenly strained into tension, and then fell slack. My face flushed; I let my head slip sideways, so that my left cheek was against the back of the chair. Through my drooping eyelashes I could see the snake-like glitter of his eyes as he stood over me. I shuddered and sighed. I was like someone fighting in vain against the sweet seduction of an overwhelming and fatal drug. I wanted to entreat him to go away, to rid me of the exquisite and sinister enchantment. But I could not speak. I shut my eyes. This was love.

The next moment I heard the soft sound of his feet on the carpet. I opened my eyes. He had stepped back. When our glances met he averted his face, and went briskly for his overcoat, which lay on the floor by the piano. I rose freed, re-established in my self-control. I arranged his collar, straightened his necktie with a few touches, picked up his hat, pushed back the crown, which flew up with a noise like a small explosion, and gave it into his hands.

'Thank you,' he said. 'To-morrow morning, eh? I shall get to know everything necessary before I come. And then we will fix things up.'

'Yes,' I said.

'I can let myself out,' he said.

I made a vague gesture, intended to signify that I could not think of permitting him to let himself out. We left the drawing-room, and passed, with precautions of silence, to the front-door, which I gently opened.

'Good-night, then,' he whispered formally, almost coldly.

I nodded. We neither of us even smiled.

We were grave, stern, and stiff in our immense self-consciousness.

'Too late for the lift,' I murmured out there with him in the vast, glittering silence of the many-angled staircase, which disappeared above us and below us into the mysterious unseen.

He nodded as I had nodded, and began to descend the broad, carpeted steps, firmly, carefully, and neither quick nor slow. I leaned over the baluster. When the turns of the staircase brought him opposite and below me, he stopped and raised his hat, and we exchanged a smile. Then he resolutely dropped his eyes and resumed the descent. From time to time I had glimpses of parts of his figure as he passed story after story. Then I heard his tread on the tessellated pavement of the main hall, the distant clatter of double doors, and a shrill cab-whistle.

This was love, at last—the reality of love! He would have killed himself had he failed to win me—killed himself! With the novelist's habit, I ran off into a series of imagined scenes—the dead body, with the hole in the temples and the awkward attitude of death; the discovery, the rush for the police, the search for a motive, the inquest, the rapid-speaking coroner, who spent his whole life at inquests; myself, cold and impassive, giving evidence, and Mary listening to what I said.... But he lived, with his delicate physical charm, his frail distinction, his spiritual grace; and he had won me. The sense of mutual possession was inexpressibly sweet to me. And it was all I had in the world now. When my mind moved from that rock, all else seemed shifting, uncertain, perilous, bodeful, and steeped in woe. The air was thick with disasters, and injustice, and strange griefs immediately I loosed my hold on the immense fact that he was mine.

'How calm I am!' I thought.

It was not till I had been in bed some three hours that I fully realized the seismic upheaval which my soul had experienced.

III

I woke up from one of those dozes which, after a sleepless night, give the brief illusion of complete rest, all my senses sharpened, and my mind factitiously active. And I began at once to anticipate Frank's coming, and to arrange rapidly my plans for closing the flat. I had determined that it should be closed. Then someone knocked at the door, and it occurred to me that there must have been a previous knock, which had, in fact, wakened me. Save on special occasions, I was never wakened, and Emmeline and my maid had injunctions not to come to me until I rang. My thoughts ran instantly to Frank. He had arrived thus early, merely because he could not keep away.

'How extremely indiscreet of him!' I thought. 'What detestable prevarications with Emmeline this will lead to! I cannot possibly be ready in time if he is to be in and out all day.'

Nevertheless, the prospect of seeing him quickly, and the idea of his splendid impatience, drenched me with joy.

'What is it?' I called out.

Emmeline entered in that terrible mauve dressing-gown which I had been powerless to persuade her to discard.

'So sorry to disturb you,' said Emmeline, feeling her loose golden hair with one hand, 'but Mrs. Ispenlove has called, and wants to see you at once. I'm afraid something has happened.'

'*Mrs.* Ispenlove?'

My voice shook.

'Yes. Yvonne came to my room and told me that Mrs. Ispenlove was here, and was either mad or very unwell, and would I go to her? So I got up at once. What shall I do? Perhaps it's something very serious. Not half-past eight, and calling like this!'

'Let her come in here immediately,' I said, turning my head on the pillow, so that Emmeline should not see the blush which had spread over my face and my neck.

It was inevitable that a terrible and desolating scene must pass between Mary Ispenlove and myself. I could not foresee how I should emerge from it, but I desperately resolved that I would suffer the worst without a moment's delay, and that no conceivable appeal should induce me to abandon Frank. I was, as I waited for Mrs. Ispenlove to appear, nothing but an embodied and fierce instinct to guard what I had won. No consideration of mercy could have touched me.

She entered with a strange, hysterical cry:

'Carlotta!'

I had asked her long ago to use my Christian name—long before I ever imagined what would come to pass between her husband and me; but I always called her Mrs. Ispenlove. The difference in our ages justified me. And that morning the difference seemed to be increased. I realized, with a cruel justice of perception quite new in my estimate of her, that she was old—an old woman. She had never been beautiful, but she was tall and graceful, and her face had been attractive by the sweetness of the mouth and the gray beneficence of the eyes; and now that sweetness and that beneficence appeared suddenly to have been swallowed up in the fatal despair of a woman who discovers that she has lived too long. Gray hair, wrinkles, crow's-feet, tired eyes, drawn mouth, and the terrible tell-tale hollow under the chin—these were what I saw in Mary Ispenlove. She had learnt that the only thing worth having in life is youth. I possessed everything that she lacked. Surely the struggle was unequal. Fate might have chosen a less piteous victim. I felt profoundly sorry for Mary Ispenlove, and this sorrow was stronger in me even than the uneasiness, the false shame (for it was not a real shame) which I experienced in her presence. I put out my hands towards her, as it were, involuntarily. She sprang to me, took them, and kissed me as I lay in bed.

'How beautiful you look—like that!' she exclaimed wildly, and with a hopeless and acute envy in her tone.

'But why—' I began to protest, astounded.

'What will you think of me, disturbing you like this? What will you think?' she moaned. And then her voice rose: 'I could not help it; I couldn't, really. Oh, Carlotta! you are my friend, aren't you?'

One thing grew swiftly clear to me: that she was as yet perfectly unaware of the relations between Frank and myself. My brain searched hurriedly for an explanation of the visit. I was conscious of an extraordinary relief.

'You are my friend, aren't you?' she repeated insistently.

Her tears were dropping on my bosom. But could I answer that I was her friend? I did not wish to be her enemy; she and Frank and I were dolls in the great hands of fate, irresponsible, guiltless, meet for an understanding sympathy. Why was I not still her friend? Did not my heart bleed for her? Yet such is the power of convention over honourableness that I could not bring myself to reply directly, 'Yes, I am your friend.'

'We have known each other a long time,' I ventured.

'There was no one else I could come to,' she said.

Her whole frame was shaking. I sat up, and asked her to pass my dressing-gown, which I put round my shoulders. Then I rang the bell.

'What are you going to do?' she demanded fearfully.

'I am going to have the gas-stove lighted and some tea brought in, and then we will talk.

Take your hat off, dear, and sit down in that chair. You'll be more yourself after a cup of tea.'

How young I was then! I remember my naïve satisfaction in this exhibition of tact. I was young and hard, as youth is apt to be—hard in spite of the compassion, too intellectual and arrogant, which I conceived for her. And even while I forbade her to talk until she had drunk some tea, I regretted the delay, and I suffered by it. Surely, I thought, she will read in my demeanour something which she ought not to read there. But she did not. She was one of the simplest of women. In ten thousand women one is born without either claws or second-sight. She was that one, defenceless as a rabbit.

'You are very kind to me,' she said, putting her cup on the mantelpiece with a nervous rattle; 'and I need it.'

'Tell me,' I murmured. 'Tell me—what I can do.'

I had remained in bed; she was by the fireplace. A distance between us seemed necessary.

'You can't do anything, my dear,' she said. 'Only I was obliged to talk to someone, after all the night. It's about Frank.'

'Mr. Ispenlove!' I ejaculated, acting as well as I could, but not very well.

'Yes. He has left me.'

'But why? What is the matter?'

Even to recall my share in this interview with Mary Ispenlove humiliates me. But perhaps I have learned the value of humiliation. Still, could I have behaved differently?

'You won't understand unless I begin a long time ago,' said Mary Ispenlove. 'Carlotta, my married life has been awful—awful—a tragedy. It has been a tragedy both for him and for me. But no one has suspected it; we have hidden it.'

I nodded. I, however, had suspected it.

'It's just twenty years—yes, twenty—since I fell in love,' she proceeded, gazing at me with her soft, moist eyes.

'With—Frank,' I assumed. I lay back in bed.

'No,' she said. 'With another man. That was in Brixton, when I was a girl living with my father; my mother was dead. He was a barrister—I mean the man I was in love with. He had only just been called to the Bar. I think everybody knew that I had fallen in love with him. Certainly he did; he could not help seeing it. I could not conceal it. Of course I can understand now that it flattered him. Naturally it did. Any man is flattered when a woman falls in love with him. And my father was rich, and so on, and so on. We saw each other a lot. I hoped, and I kept on hoping. Some people even said it was a match, and that I was throwing myself away. Fancy—throwing myself away—me!—who have never been good for anything! My father did not care much for the man; said he was selfish and grasping. Possibly he was; but I was in love with him all the same. Then I met Frank, and Frank fell in love with me. You know how obstinate Frank is when he has once set his mind on a thing. Frank determined to have me; and my father was on his side. I would not listen. I didn't give him so much as a chance to propose to me. And this state of things lasted for quite a long time. It wasn't my fault; it wasn't anybody's fault.'

'Just so,' I agreed, raising my head on one elbow, and listening intently. It was the first sincere word I had spoken, and I was glad to utter it.

'The man I had fallen in love with came nearer. He was decidedly tempted. I began to feel sure of him. All I wanted was to marry him, whether he loved me a great deal or only a little tiny bit. I was in that state. Then he drew away. He scarcely ever came to the house, and I seemed never to be able to meet him. And then one day my father showed me something in the *Morning Post*. It was a paragraph saying that the man I was in love with was going to marry a woman of title, a widow and the daughter of a peer. I soon found out she was nearly twice his age. He had done it to get on. He was getting on very well by himself, but I suppose that wasn't fast enough for him. Carlotta, it nearly killed me. And I felt so sorry for him. You can't guess how sorry I felt for him. I felt that he didn't know what he had missed. Oh, how happy I should have made him! I should have lived for him. I should have done everything for him. I should have ... You don't mind me telling you all this?'

I made an imploring gesture.

'What a shame!' I burst out.

'Ah, my dear!' she said, 'he didn't love me. One can't blame him.'

'And then?' I questioned, with an eagerness that I tried to overcome.

'Frank was so persevering. And—and—I *did* admire his character. A woman couldn't help admiring his character, could she? And, besides, I honestly thought I had got over the other affair, and that I was in love with him. I refused him once, and then I married him. He was as mad for me as I had been for the other one. Yes, I married him, and we both imagined we were going to be happy.'

'And why haven't you been?' I asked.

'This is my shame,' she said. 'I could not forget the other one. We soon found that out.'

'Did you *talk* about it, you—and Frank?' I put in, amazed.

'Oh *no*!' she said. 'It was never mentioned—never once during fifteen years. But he knew; and I knew that he knew. The other one was always between us—always, always, always! The other one was always in my heart. We did our best, both of us; but it was useless. The passion of my life was—it was invincible. I *tried* to love Frank. I could only like him. Fancy his position! And we were helpless. Because, you know, Frank and I are not the sort of people that go and make a scandal—at least, that was what I thought,' she sighed. 'I know different now. Well, he died the day before yesterday.'

'Who?'

'Crettell. He had just been made a judge. He was the youngest judge on the bench—only forty-six.'

'Was *that* the man?' I exclaimed; for Crettell's character was well known in London.

'That was the man. Frank came in yesterday afternoon, and after he had glanced at the paper, he said: "By the way, Crettell's dead." I did not grasp it at first. He repeated: "Crettell—he's dead." I burst into tears. I couldn't help it. And, besides, I forgot. Frank asked me very roughly what I was crying for. You know, Frank has much changed these last few months. He is not as nice as he used to be. Excuse me talking like this, my dear. Something must be worrying him. Well, I said as well as I could while I was crying that the news was a shock to me. I tried to stop crying, but I couldn't. I sobbed. Frank threw down the paper and stamped on it, and he swore. He said: "I know you've always been in love with the brute, but you needn't make such a damn fuss about it." Oh, my dear, how can I tell you these things? That angered me. This was the first time in our married life that Crettell had been even referred to, and it seemed to me that Frank put all the hatred of fifteen years into that single sentence. Why was I angry? I didn't know. We had a scene. Frank lost his temper, for the first time that I remember, and then he recovered it. He said quietly he couldn't stand living with me any more; and that he had long since wanted to leave me. He said he would never see me again. And then one of the servants came in, and—'

'What?'

'Nothing. I sent her out. And—and—Fran didn't come home last night.'

There was a silence. I could find nothing to say, and Mary had hidden her face. I utterly forgot myself and my own state in this extraordinary hazard of matrimony. I could only think of Mary's grief—a grief which, nevertheless, I did not too well comprehend.

'Then you love him now?' I ventured at length.

She made no reply.

'You love him—is that so?' I pursued. 'Tell me honestly.'

I spoke as gently as it was in me to speak.

'Honestly!' she cried, looking up. 'Honestly! No! If I loved him, could I have been so upset about Crettell? But we have been together so long. We are husband and wife, Carlotta. We are so used to each other. And generally he is so good. We've got on very well, considering. And now he's left me. Think of the scandal! It will be terrible! terrible! A separation at my age! Carlotta, it's unthinkable! He's mad—that's the only explanation. Haven't I tried to be a good wife to him? He's never found fault with me— never! And I'm sure, as regards him, I've had nothing to complain of.'

'He will come back,' I said. 'He'll think things over and see reason.'

And it was just as though I heard some other person saying these words.

'But he didn't come *home* last night,' Mary insisted. 'What the servants are thinking I shouldn't like to guess.'

'What does it matter what the servants think?' I said brusquely.

'But it *does* matter. He didn't come *home*. He must have slept at a hotel. Fancy, sleeping at a hotel, and his home waiting for him! Oh, Carlotta, you're too young to understand what I feel! You're very clever, and you're very sympathetic; but you can't see things as I see them. Wait till you've been married fifteen years. The scandal! The shame! And me only too anxious to be a good wife, and to keep our home as it should be, and to help him as much as I can with my stupid brains in his business!'

'I can understand perfectly,' I asserted. 'I can understand perfectly.'

And I could. The futility of arguing with Mary, of attempting to free her ever so little from the coils of convention which had always bound her, was only too plainly apparent. She was—and naturally, sincerely, instinctively—the very incarnation and mouthpiece of the conventionality of society, as she cowered there in her grief and her quiet resentment. But this did not impair the authenticity of her grief and her resentment.

Her grief appealed to me powerfully, and her resentment, almost angelic in its quality, seemed sufficiently justified. I knew that my own position was in practice untenable, that logic must always be inferior to emotion. I am intensely proud of my ability to see, then, that no sentiment can be false which is sincere, and that Mary Ispenlove's attitude towards marriage was exactly as natural, exactly as free from artificiality, as my own. Can you go outside Nature? Is not the polity of Londoners in London as much a part of Nature as the polity of bees in a hive?

'Not a word for fifteen years, and then an explosion like that!' she murmured, incessantly recurring to the core of her grievance. 'I did wrong to marry him, I know. But I *did* marry him—I *did* marry him! We are husband and wife. And he goes off and sleeps at a hotel! Carlotta, I wish I had never been born! What will people say? I shall never be able to look anyone in the face again.'

'He will come back,' I said again.

'Do you think so?'

This time she caught at the straw.

'Yes,' I said. 'And you will settle down gradually; and everything will be forgotten.'

I said that because it was the one thing I could say. I repeat that I had ceased to think of myself. I had become a spectator.

'It can never be the same between us again,' Mary breathed sadly.

At that moment Emmeline Palmer plunged, rather than came, into my bedroom.

'Oh, Miss Peel—' she began, and then stopped, seeing Mrs. Ispenlove by the fireplace, though she knew that Mrs. Ispenlove was with me.

'Anything wrong?' I asked, affecting a complete calm.

It was evident that the good creature had lost her head, as she sometimes did, when I gave her too much to copy, or when the unusual occurred in no matter what form. The excellent Emmeline was one of my mistakes.

'Mr. Ispenlove is here,' she whispered.

None of us spoke for a few seconds. Mary Ispenlove stared at me, but whether in terror or astonishment, I could not guess. This was one of the most dramatic moments of my life.

'Tell Mr. Ispenlove that I can see nobody,' I said, glancing at the wall.

She turned to go.

'And, Emmeline,' I stopped her. 'Do not tell him anything else.'

Surely the fact that Frank had called to see me before nine o'clock in the morning, surely my uneasy demeanour, must at length arouse suspicion even in the simple, trusting mind of his wife!

'How does he know that I am here?' Mary asked, lowering her voice, when

Emmeline had shut the door; 'I said nothing to the servants.'

I was saved. Her own swift explanation of his coming was, of course, the most natural in the world. I seized on it.

'Never mind how,' I answered. 'Perhaps he was watching outside your house, and followed you. The important thing is that he has come. It proves,' I went on, inventing rapidly, 'that he has changed his mind and recognises his mistake. Had you not better go back home as quickly as you can? It would have been rather awkward for you to see him here, wouldn't it?'

'Yes, yes,' she said, her eyes softening and gleaming with joy. 'I will go. Oh, Carlotta! how can I thank you? You are my best friend.'

'I have done nothing,' I protested. But I had.

'You are a dear!' she exclaimed, coming impulsively to the bed.

I sat up. She kissed me fervently. I rang the bell.

'Has Mr. Ispenlove gone?' I asked Emmeline.

'Yes,' said Emmeline.

In another minute his wife, too, had departed, timorously optimistic, already denying in her heart that it could never be the same between them again. She assuredly would not find Frank at home. But that was nothing. I had escaped! I had escaped!

'Will you mind getting dressed at once?' I said to Emmeline. 'I should like you to go out with a letter and a manuscript as soon as possible.'

I got a notebook and began to write to Frank. I told him all that had happened, in full detail, writing hurriedly, in gusts, and abandoning that regard for literary form which the professional author is apt to preserve even in his least formal correspondence.

'After this,' I said, 'we must give up what we decided last night. I have no good reason to offer you. The situation itself has not been changed by what I have learnt from your wife. I have not even discovered that she loves you, though in spite of what she says, which I have faithfully told you, I fancy she does—at any rate, I think she is beginning to. My ideas about the rights of love are not changed. My feelings towards you are not changed. Nothing is changed. But she and I have been through that interview, and so, after all, everything is changed; we must give it all up. You will say I am illogical. I am—perhaps. It was a mere chance that your wife came to me. I don't know why she did. If she had not come, I should have given myself to you. Supposing she had written—I should still have given myself to you. But I have been in her presence. I have been with her. And then the thought that you struck her, for my sake! She said nothing about that. That was the one thing she concealed. I could have cried when she passed it over. After all, I don't know whether it is sympathy for your wife that makes me change, or my self-respect—say my self-pride; I'm a proud woman. I lied to her through all that interview.

'Oh, if I had only had the courage to begin by telling her outright and bluntly that you and I had settled that I should take her place! That would have stopped her. But I hadn't. And, besides, how could I foresee what she would say to me and how she would affect me? No; I lied to her at every point. My whole attitude was a lie. Supposing you and I had gone off together before I had seen her, and then I had met her afterwards, I could have looked her in the face—sorrowfully, with a heart bleeding—but I could have looked her in the face. But after this interview—no; it would be impossible for me to face her with you at my side! Don't I put things crudely, horribly! I know everything that you will say. You could not bring a single argument that I have not thought of.

'However, arguments are nothing. It is how I feel. Fate is against us. Possibly I have ruined your life and mine without having done anything to improve hers; and possibly I have saved us all three from terrible misery. Possibly fate is with us. No one can say. I don't know what will happen in the immediate future; I won't think about it. If you do as I wish, if you have any desire to show me that I have any influence over you, you will go back to live with your wife. Where did you sleep last night? Or did you walk the streets? You must not answer this letter at present. Write to me later. Do not try to see me. I won't see you. We *mustn't* meet. I am going away at once. I don't think I could stand another scene with your wife, and she would be sure to come again to me.

'Try to resume your old existence. You can do it if you try. Remember that your wife is no more to blame than you are, or than I am. Remember that you loved her once. And remember that I act as I am acting because there is no other way for me. *C'est plus fort que moi,* I am going to Torquay. I let you know this—I hate concealment; and anyway you would find out. But I shall trust you not to follow me. I shall trust you. You are saying that this is a very different woman from last night. It is. I haven't yet realized what my feelings are. I expect I shall realize them in a few days. I send with this a manuscript. It is nothing. I send it merely to put Emmeline off the scent, so that she shall think that it is purely business. Now I shall *trust* you.—C. P.'

I commenced the letter without even a 'Dear Frank,' and I ended it without an affectionate word.

'I should like you to take these down to Mr. Ispenlove's office,' I said to Emmeline. 'Ask for him and give them to him yourself. There's no answer. He's pretty sure to be in. But if he isn't, bring them back. I'm going to Torquay by that eleven-thirty express—isn't it?'

'Eleven-thirty-five,' Emmeline corrected me coldly.

When she returned, she said she had seen Mr. Ispenlove and given him the letter and the parcel.

IV

I had acquaintances in Torquay, but I soon discovered that the place was impossible for me. Torquay is the chosen home of the proprieties, the respectabilities, and all the conventions. Nothing could dislodge them from its beautiful hills; the very sea, as it beats primly, or with a violence that never forgets to be discreet, on the indented shore, acknowledges their sway. Aphrodite never visits there; the human race is not continued there. People who have always lived within the conventions go there to die within the conventions. The young do not flourish there; they escape from the soft enervation. Since everybody is rich, there are no poor. There are only the rich, and the servitors, who get rich. These two classes never mix—even in the most modest villas they live on opposite sides of the house. The life of the town is a vast conspiracy on the part of the servitors to guard against any danger of the rich taking all their riches to heaven. You can, if you are keen enough, detect portions of this conspiracy in every shop. On the hills each abode stands in its own undulating grounds, is approached by a winding drive of at least ten yards, is wrapped about by the silence of elms, is flanked by greenhouses, and exudes an immaculate propriety from all its windows. In the morning the rich descend, the servitors ascend; the bosky and perfectly-kept streets on the hills are trodden with apologetic celerity by the emissaries of the servitors. The one interminable thoroughfare of the town is graciously invaded by the rich, who, if they have not walked down for the sake of exercise, step cautiously from their carriages, enunciate a string of orders ending with the name of a house, and cautiously regain their carriages. Each house has a name, and the pride of the true servitor is his ability to deduce instantly from the name of the house the name of its owner and the name of its street. In the afternoon a vast and complicated game of visiting cards is played. One does not begin to be serious till the evening; one eats then, solemnly and fully, to the faint accompaniment of appropriate conversation. And there is no relief, no surcease from utmost conventionality. It goes on night and day; it hushes one to sleep, and wakes one up. On all but the strongest minds it casts a narcotizing spell, so that thought is arrested, and originality, vivacity, individuality become a crime—a shame that must be hidden. Into this strange organism I took my wounded heart, imagining that an atmosphere of coma might help to heal it. But no! Within a week my state had become such that I could have cried out in mid Union Street at noon: 'Look at me with your dead eyes, you dead who have omitted to get buried, I am among you, and I am an adulteress in spirit! And my body has sinned the sin! And I am alive as only grief can be alive. I suffer the torture of vultures, but I would not exchange my lot with yours!'

And one morning, after a fortnight, I thought of Monte Carlo. And the vision of that place, which I had never seen, too voluptuously lovely to be really beautiful, where there are no commandments, where unconventionality and conventionality fight it out on even terms, where the adulteress swarms, and the sin is for ever sinned, and wounded hearts go about gaily, where it is impossible to distinguish between virtue and vice, and where Toleration in fine clothes is the supreme social goddess—the vision of Monte Carlo, as a place of refuge from the exacerbating and moribund and yet eternal demureness of Torquay, appealed to me so persuasively that I was on my way to the Riviera in two hours. In that crisis of my life my moods were excessively capricious. Let me say that I had not reached Exeter before I began to think kindly of Torquay. What was Torquay but an almost sublime example of what the human soul can accomplish in its unending quest of an ideal?

I left England on a calm, slate-coloured sea—sea that more than any other sort of sea produces the reflective melancholy which makes wonderful the faces of fishermen. How that brief voyage symbolized for me the mysterious movement of humanity! We converged from the four quarters of the universe, passed together an hour, helpless, in somewhat inimical curiosity concerning each other, and then, mutually forgotten, took wing, and spread out into the unknown. I think that as I stood near the hot funnel, breasting the wind, and vacantly staring at the smooth expanse that continually slipped from under us, I understood myself better than I had done before. My soul was at peace—the peace of ruin after a conflagration, but peace. Sometimes a little flame would dart out—flame of regret, revolt, desire—and I would ruthlessly extinguish it. I felt that I had nothing to live for, that no energy remained to me, no interest, no hope. I saw the forty years of probable existence in front of me flat and sterile as the sea itself. I was coldly glad that I had finished my novel, well knowing that it would be my last. And the immense disaster had been caused by a chance! Why had I been born with a vein of overweening honesty in me? Why should I have sacrificed everything to the pride of my conscience, seeing that consciences were the product of education merely? Useless to try to answer the unanswerable! What is, is. And circumstances are always at the mercy of character. I might have been wrong, I might have been right; no ethical argument could have bent my instinct. I did not sympathize with myself—I was too proud and stern—but I sympathized with Frank. I wished ardently that he might be consoled—that his agony might not be too terrible. I wondered where he was, what he was doing. I had received no letter from him, but then I had instructed that letters should not be forwarded to me. My compassion went out after him, followed him into the dark, found him (as I hoped), and surrounded him like an alleviating influence. I thought pityingly of the ravage that had been occasioned by our love. His home was wrecked. Our lives were equally wrecked. Our friends were grieved; they would think sadly of my closed flat. Even the serio-comic figure of Emmeline touched me; I had paid her three months' wages and dismissed her. Where would she go with her mauve *peignoir*? She was over thirty, and would not easily fall into another such situation. Imagine Emmeline struck down by a splinter from our passionate explosion! Only Yvonne was content at the prospect of revisiting France.

'Ah! *Qu'on est bien ici, madame*!' she said, when we had fixed ourselves in the long and glittering *train de grand luxe* that awaited us at Calais. Once I had enjoyed luxury, but now the futility of all this luxurious cushioned arrogance, which at its best only corresponded with a railway director's dreams of paradise, seemed to me pathetic. Could it detain youth, which is for ever flying? Could it keep out sorrow? Could it breed hope? As the passengers, so correct in their travelling costumes, passed to and fro in the corridors with the subdued murmurs always adopted by English people when they wish to prove that they are not excited, I thought: 'Does it matter how you and I go southwards? The pride of the eye, and of the palate, and of the limbs, what can it help us that this should be sated? We cannot leave our souls behind.' The history of many of these men and women was written on their faces. I wondered if my history was written on mine, gazing into the mirrors which were everywhere, but seeing nothing save that which I had always seen. Then I smiled, and Yvonne smiled respectfully in response. Was I not part of the immense pretence that riches bring joy and that life is good? On every table in the restaurant-cars were bunches of fresh flowers that had been torn from the South, and would return there dead, having ministered to the illusion that riches bring joy and that life is good. I hated that. I could almost have wished that I was travelling southwards in a slow, slow train, third class, where sorrow at any rate does not wear a mask. Great grief is democratic, levelling—not downwards but upwards. It strips away the inessential, and makes brothers. It is impatient with all the unavailing inventions which obscure the brotherhood of mankind.

I descended from the train restlessly—there were ten minutes to elapse before the departure—and walked along the platform, glimpsing the faces in the long procession of windows, and then the flowers and napery in the two restaurant-cars: wistful all alike, I thought—flowers and faces! How fanciful, girlishly fanciful, I was! Opposite the door of the first car stood a gigantic negro in the sober blue and crimson livery of the International Sleeping Car Company. He wore white gloves, like all the servants on the train: it was to foster the illusion; it was part of what we paid for.

'When is luncheon served?' I asked him idly.

He looked massively down at me as I shivered slightly in my furs. He contemplated me for an instant. He seemed to add me up, antipathetically, as a product of Western civilization.

'Soon as the train starts, madam,' he replied suavely, in good American, and resumed nonchalantly his stare into the distance of the platform.

'Thank you!' I said.

I was glad that I had encountered him on that platform and not in the African bush. I speculated upon the chain of injustice and oppression that had warped his destiny from what it ought to have been to what it was. 'And he, too, is human, and knows love and grief and illusion, like me,' I mused. A few yards further on the engine-driver and stoker were busy with coal and grease. 'Five minutes hence, and our lives, and our correctness, and our luxury, will be in their grimy hands,' I said to myself. Strange world, the world of the *train de grand luxe*! But a world of brothers! I regained my carriage, exactly, after all, as the inhabitants of Torquay regained theirs.

Then the wondrous self-contained microcosm, shimmering with gilt and varnish and crystal, glorious in plush and silk, heavy with souls and all that correct souls could possibly need in twenty hours, gathered itself up and rolled forward, swiftly, and more swiftly, into the wide, gray landscapes of France. The vibrating and nerve-destroying monotony of a long journey had commenced. We were summoned by white gloves to luncheon; and we lunched in a gliding palace where the heavenly dreams of a railway director had received their most luscious expression—and had then been modestly hidden by advertisements of hotels and brandy.

The Southern flowers shook in their slender glasses, and white gloves balanced dishes as if on board ship, and the electric fans revolved ceaselessly. As I was finishing my meal, a middle-aged woman whom I knew came down the car towards me. She had evidently not recognised me.

'How do you do, Miss Kate?' I accosted her.

It was the younger of Vicary's two maiden sisters. I guessed that the other could not be far away.

She hesitated, stopped, and looked down at me, rather as the negro had done.

'Oh! how do you do, Miss Peel?' she said distantly, with a nervous simper; and she passed on.

This was my first communication, since my disappearance, with the world of my London friends and acquaintances. I perceived, of course, from Miss Kate's attitude that something must have occurred, or something must have been assumed, to my prejudice. Perhaps Frank had also vanished for a time, and the rumour ran that we were away together. I smiled frigidly. What matter? In case Miss Vicary should soon be following her sister, I left without delay and went back to my coupé; it would have been a pity to derange these dames. Me away with Frank! What folly to suppose it! Yet it might have been. I was in heart what these dames probably took me for. I read a little in the *Imitation of Christ* which Aunt Constance had meant to give me, that book which will survive sciences and even Christianity itself. 'Think not that thou hast made any progress,' I read, 'unless thou feel thyself inferior to all ... Behold how far off thou art yet from true charity and humility: which knows not how to be angry or indignant, with any except one's self.'

Night fell. The long, illuminated train roared and flashed on its invisible way under a dome of stars. It shrieked by mysterious stations, dragging furiously its freight of luxury and light and human masks through placid and humble villages and towns, of which it ignored everything save their coloured signals of safety. Ages of oscillation seemed to pass. In traversing the corridors one saw interior after interior full of the signs of wearied humanity: magazines thrown aside, rugs in disorder, hair dishevelled, eyes heavy, cheeks flushed, limbs in the abandoned attitudes of fatigue—here and there a compartment with blinds discreetly drawn, suggesting the jealous seclusion of love, and here and there a group of animated tatlers or card-players whose nerves nothing could affect, and who were incapable of lassitude; on every train and every steamer a few such are to be found.

More ages passed, and yet the journey had but just begun. At length we thundered and resounded through canyons of tall houses, their façades occasionally bathed in the cold, blue radiance of arc-lights; and under streets and over canals. Paris! the city of the joy of life! We were to see the muddied skirts of that brilliant and sinister woman. We panted to a standstill in the vast echoing cavern of the Gare du Nord, stared haughtily and drowsily at its bustling confusion, and then drew back, to carry our luxury and our correctness through the lowest industrial quarters. Belleville, Menilmontant, and other names of like associations we read on the miserable, forlorn stations of the Ceinture, past which we trailed slowly our disgust.

We made a semicircle through the secret shames that beautiful Paris would fain hide, and, emerging, found ourselves in the deserted and stony magnificence of the Gare de Lyon, the gate of the South. Here, where we were not out of keeping, where our splendour was of a piece with the splendour of the proudest terminus in France, we rested long, fretted by the inexplicable leisureliness on the part of a *train de grand luxe*, while gilded officials paced to and fro beneath us on the platforms, guarding in their bureaucratic breasts the secret of the exact instant at which the great express would leave. I slept, and dreamed that the Misses Vicary had brought several pairs of white gloves in order to have me dismissed from the society of the train. A hand touched me. It was Yvonne's. I awoke to a renewal of the maddening vibration. We had quitted Paris long since. It was after seven o'clock. '*On dit que le diner est servi, madame* said Yvonne. I told her to go, and I collected my wits to follow her. As I was emerging into the corridor, Miss Kate went by. I smiled faintly, perhaps timidly. She cut me completely. Then I went out into the corridor. A man was standing at the other end twirling his moustaches. He turned round.

It was Frank.

He came towards me, uncertainly swaying with the movement of the swaying train.

'Good God!' he muttered, and stopped within a yard of me.

I clung convulsively to the framework of the doorway. Our lives paused.

'Why have you followed me, Frank?' I asked gloomily, in a whisper.

I had meant to be severe, offended. I had not meant to put his name at the end of my question, much less to utter it tenderly, like an endearment. But I had little control over myself. I was almost breathless with a fatal surprise, shaken with terrible emotion.

'I've not followed you,' he said. 'I joined the train at Paris. I'd no idea you were on the train till I saw you in the corner asleep, through the window of the compartment. I've been waiting here till you came out.'

'Have you seen the Vicarys?'

'Yes,' he answered.

'Ah! You've been away from London all this time?'

'I couldn't stay. I couldn't. I've been in Belgium and Holland. Then I went to Paris. And now—you see me.'

'I'm going to Mentone,' I said. 'I had thought of Monte Carlo first, but

I changed my mind. Where are you going to?'

'Mentone,' he said.

We talked in hard, strained tones, avoiding each other's eyes. A string of people passed along the car on their way to dinner. I withdrew into my compartment, and Frank flattened himself against a window.

'Come in here a minute,' I said, when they were gone.

He entered the compartment and sat down opposite to me and lifted his hand, perhaps unconsciously, to pull the door to.

'No,' I said; 'don't shut it. Leave it like that.'

He was dressed in a gray tourist suit. Never before had I seen him in any but the formal attire of London. I thought he looked singularly graceful and distinguished, even romantic, in that loose, soft clothing. But no matter what he wore, Frank satisfied the eye. We were both extremely nervous and excited and timid, fearing speech.

'Carlotta,' he said at last—I had perceived that he was struggling to a resolution—'this is the best thing that could have happened. Whatever we do, everybody will believe that we are running off together.'

'I think they have been believing that ever since we left London,' I said; and I told him about Miss Kate's treatment of me at lunch. 'But how can that affect us?' I demanded.

'Mary will believe it—does believe, I'm sure. Long before this, people will have enlightened her. And now the Vicarys have seen us, it's all over. Our hand is forced, isn't it?'

'Frank,' I said, 'didn't you think my letter was right?'

'I obeyed it,' he replied heavily. 'I haven't even written to you. I meant to when I got to Mentone.'

'But didn't you think I was right?'

'I don't know. Yes—I suppose it was.' His lower lip fell. 'Of course I don't want you to do anything that you—'

'Dinner, please,' said my negro, putting his head between us.

We both informed the man that we should not dine, and I asked him to tell

Yvonne not to wait for me.

'There's your maid, too,' said Frank. 'How are we going to get out of it?

The thing's settled for us.'

'My dear, dear boy!' I exclaimed. 'Are we to outrage our consciences simply because people think we have outraged them?'

'It isn't my conscience—it's yours,' he said.

'Well, then—mine.'

I drew down my veil; I could scarcely keep dry eyes.

'Why are you so hard, Carlotta?' he cried. 'I can't understand you. I never could. But you'll kill me—that's what you'll do.'

Impulsively I leaned forward; and he seized my hand. Our antagonism melted in tears. Oh the cruel joy of that moment! Who will dare to say that the spirit cannot burn with pleasure while drowning in grief? Or that tragedy may not be the highest bliss? That instant of renunciation was our true marriage. I realize it now—a union that nothing can soil nor impair.

'I love you; you are fast and fast in my heart,' I murmured. 'But you must go back to Mary. There is nothing else.'

And I withdrew my hand.

He shook his head.

'You've no right, my dearest, to tell me to go back to Mary. I cannot.'

'Forgive me,' I said. 'I have only the right to ask you to leave me.'

'Then there is no hope?'

His lips trembled. Ah! those lips!

I made a sign that there was no hope. And we sat in silence, overcome.

A servant came to arrange the compartment for sleeping, and we were obliged to assume nonchalance and go into the corridor. All the windows of the corridor were covered with frost traceries. The train with its enclosed heat and its gleaming lamps was plunging through an ice-gripped night. I thought of the engine-driver, perched on his shaking, snorting, monstrous machine, facing the weather, with our lives and our loves in his hand.

'We'll leave each other now, Frank,' I said, 'before the people begin to come back from dinner. Go and eat something.'

'But you?'

'I shall be all right. Yvonne will get me some fruit. I shall stay in our compartment till we arrive.'

'Yes. And when we do arrive—what then? What are your wishes? You see, I can't leave the train before we get to Mentone because of my registered luggage.'

He spoke appealingly.

The dear thing, with his transparent pretexts!

'You can ignore us at the station, and then leave Mentone again during the day.'

'As you wish,' he said.

'Good-night!' I whispered. 'Good-bye!' And I turned to my compartment.

'Carlotta!' he cried despairingly.

But I shut the door and drew the blinds.

Yvonne was discretion itself when she returned. She had surely seen Frank. No doubt she anticipated piquant developments at Mentone.

All night I lay on my narrow bed, with Yvonne faintly snoring above me, and the harsh, metallic rattle of the swinging train beneath. I could catch the faint ticking of my watch under the thin pillow. The lamp burnt delicately within its green shade. I lay almost moveless, almost dead, shifting only at long intervals from side to side. Sometimes my brain would arouse itself, and I would live again through each scene of my relationship with Frank and Mary. I often thought of the engine-driver, outside, watching over us and unflinchingly dragging us on. I hoped that his existence had compensations.

V

Early on the second morning after that interview in the train I sat on my balcony in the Hôtel d'Écosse, full in the tremendous sun that had ascended over the Mediterranean. The shore road wound along beneath me by the blue water that never receded nor advanced, lopping always the same stones. A vivid yellow electric tram, like a toy, crept forward on my left from the direction of Vintimille and Italy, as it were swimming noiselessly on the smooth surface of the road among the palms of an intense green, against the bright blue background of the sea; and another tram advanced, a spot of orange, to meet it out of the variegated tangle of tinted houses composing the Old Town. High upon the summit of the Old Town rose the slim, rose-coloured cupola of the church in a sapphire sky. The regular smiting sound of a cracked bell, viciously rung, came from it. The eastern prospect was shut in by the last olive-clad spurs of the Alps, that tread violently and gigantically into the sea. The pathways of the hotel garden were being gently swept by a child of the sun, who could not have sacrificed his graceful dignity to haste; and many peaceful morning activities proceeded on the road, on the shore, and on the jetty. A procession of tawny fishing-boats passed from the harbour one after another straight into the eye of the sun, and were lost there. Smoke climbed up softly into the soft air from the houses and hotels on the level of the road. The trams met and parted, silently widening the distance between them which previously they had narrowed. And the sun rose and rose, bathing the blue sea and the rich verdure and the glaring white architecture in the very fluid of essential life. The whole azure coast basked in it like an immense cat, commencing the day with a voluptuous savouring of the fact that it was alive. The sun is the treacherous and tyrannical god of the South, and when he withdraws himself, arbitrary and cruel, the land and the people shiver and prepare to die.

It was such a morning as renders sharp and unmistakable the division between body and soul—if the soul suffers. The body exults; the body cries out that nothing on earth matters except climate. Nothing can damp the glorious ecstasy of the body baptized in that air, caressed by that incomparable sun. It laughs, and it laughs at the sorrow of the soul. It imperiously bids the soul to choose the path of pleasure; it shouts aloud that sacrifice is vain and honour an empty word, full of inconveniences, and that to exist amply and vehemently, to listen to the blood as it beats strongly through the veins, is the end of the eternal purpose. Ah! how easy it is to martyrize one's self by some fatal decision made grandly in the exultation of a supreme moment! And how difficult to endure the martyrdom without regret! I regretted my renunciation. My body rebelled against it, and even my soul rebelled. I scorned myself for a fool, for a sentimental weakling—yes, and for a moral coward. Every argument that presented itself damaged the justice of my decision. After all, we loved, and in my secret dreams had I not always put love first, as the most sacred? The reality was that I had been afraid of what Mary would think. True, my attitude had lied to her, but I could not have avoided that. Decency would have forbidden me to use any other attitude; and more than decency—kindness. Ought the course of lives to be changed at the bidding of mere hazard? It was a mere chance that Mary had called on me. I bled for her grief, but nothing that I could do would assuage it. I felt sure that, in the impossible case of me being able to state my position to her and argue in its defence, I could force her to see that in giving myself to Frank I was not being false to my own ideals. What else could count? What other consideration should guide the soul on its mysterious instinctive way? Frank and I had a right to possess each other. We had a right to be happy if we could. And the one thing that had robbed us of that right was my lack of courage, caused partly by my feminine mentality (do we not realize sometimes how ignobly feminine we are?), and partly by the painful spectacle of Mary's grief.... And her grief, her most intimate grief, sprang not from thwarted love, but from a base and narrow conventionality.

Thus I declaimed to myself in my heart, under the influence of the seductive temptations of that intoxicating atmosphere.

'Come down,' said a voice firmly and quietly underneath me in the orange-trees of the garden.

I started violently. It was Frank's voice. He was standing in the garden, his legs apart, and a broad, flat straw hat, which I did not admire, on his head. His pale face was puckered round about the eyes as he looked up at me, like the face of a person trying to look directly at the sun.

'Why,' I exclaimed foolishly, glancing down over the edge of the balcony, and shutting my white parasol with a nervous, hurried movement, 'have—have you come here?'

He had disobeyed my wish. He had not left Mentone at once.

'Come down,' he repeated persuasively, and yet commandingly.

I could feel my heart beating against the marble parapet of the balcony. I seemed to be caught, to be trapped. I could not argue with him in that position. I could not leave him shouting in the garden. So I nodded to pacify him, and disappeared quickly from the balcony, almost scurrying away. And in the comparative twilight of my room I stopped and gave a glance in the mirror, and patted my hair, and fearfully examined the woman that I saw in the glass, as if to discern what sort of woman she truly was, and what was the root of her character. I hesitated and snatched up my gloves. I wanted to collect my thoughts, and I could not. It was impossible to think clearly. I moved in the room, dazed. I stood by the tumbled bed, fingering the mosquito curtains. They might have been a veil behind which was obscured the magic word of enlightenment I needed. I opened the door, shut it suddenly, and held the knob tight, defying an imagined enemy outside. 'Oh!' I muttered at last, angry with myself, 'what is the use of all this? You know you must go down to him. He's waiting for you. Show a little common-sense and go without so much fuss.' And so I descended the stairs swiftly and guiltily, relieved that no one happened to see me. In any case, I decided, nothing could induce me to yield to him after my letter and after what had passed in the train. The affair was beyond argument. I felt that I could not yield, and that though it meant the ruin of happiness by obstinacy, I could not yield. I shrank from yielding in that moment as men shrink from public repentance.

He had not moved from his post in the garden. We shook hands. A band of Italian musicians wandered into the garden and began to sing Verdi to a vigorous thrumming of guitars. They sang as only Italians can sing—as naturally as they breathed, and with a rich and overflowing innocent joy in the art which Nature had taught them. They sang loudly, swingingly, glancing full of naive hope up at the windows of the vast, unresponsive hotel.

'So you are still in Mentone,' I ventured.

'Yes,' he said. 'Come for a walk.'

'But—'

'Come for a walk.'

'Very well,' I consented. 'As I am?'

'As you are. I saw you all in white on the balcony, and I was determined to fetch you out.'

'But could you see who it was from the road?'

'Of course I could. I knew in an instant.'

We descended, he a couple of paces in front of me, the narrow zigzag path leading down between two other hotels to the shore road.

'What will happen now?' I asked myself wildly. My head swam.

It seemed that nothing would happen. We turned eastwards, walking slowly, and I began to resume my self-control. Only the simple and the humble were abroad at that early hour: purveyors of food, in cheerfully rattling carts, or hauling barrows with the help of grave and formidable dogs; washers and cleaners at the doors of highly-decorated villas, amiably performing their tasks while the mighty slept; fishermen and fat fisher-girls, industriously repairing endless brown nets on the other side of the parapet of the road; a postman and a little policeman; a porcelain mender, who practised his trade under the shadow of the wall; a few loafers; some stable-boys exercising horses; and children with adorable dirty faces, shouting in their high treble as they played at hopscotch. I felt very closely akin to these meek ones as we walked along. They were so human, so wistful. They had the wonderful simplicity of animals, uncomplicated by the disease of self-consciousness; they were the vital stuff without the embroidery. They preserved the customs of their ancestors, rising with the sun, frankly and splendidly enjoying the sun, looking up to it as the most important thing in the world. They never attempted to understand what was beyond them; they troubled not with progress, ideals, righteousness, the claims of society. They accepted humbly and uninquiringly what they found. They lived the life of their instincts, sometimes violent, often kindly, and always natural. Why should I have felt so near to them?

A calm and gentle pleasure filled me, far from intense, but yet satisfying. I determined to enjoy the moment, or, perhaps, without determination, I gave myself up, gradually, to the moment. I forgot care and sorrow. I was well; I was with Frank; I was in the midst of enchanting natural beauty; the day was fair and fresh and virgin. I knew not where I was going. Shorewards a snowy mountain ridge rose above the long, wide slopes of olives, dotted with white dwellings. A single sail stood up seawards on the immense sheet of blue. The white sail appeared and disappeared in the green palm-trees as we passed eastwards. Presently we left the sea, and we lost the hills, and came into a street of poor little shops for simple folk, that naïvely exposed their cheap and tawdry goods to no matter what mightiness should saunter that way. And then we came to the end of the tram-line, and it was like the end of the world. And we saw in the distance abodes of famous persons, fabulously rich, defying the sea and the hills, and condescending from afar off to the humble. We crossed the railway, and a woman ran out from a cabin with a spoon in one hand and a soiled flag in the other, and waved the flag at a towering black engine that breathed stertorously in a cutting. Already we were climbing, and the road grew steeper, and then we came to custom-houses—unsightly, squalid, irregular, and mean—in front of which officials laughed and lounged and smoked.

We talked scarcely at all.

'You were up early this morning,' he said.

'Yes; I could not sleep.'

'It was the same with me.'

We recovered the sea; but now it was far below us, and the footprints of the wind were marked on it, and it was not one blue, but a thousand blues, and it faded imperceptibly into the sky. The sail, making Mentone, was much nearer, and had developed into a two-masted ship. It seemed to be pushed, rather than blown, along by the wind. It seemed to have rigidity in all its parts, and to be sliding unwillingly over a vast slate. The road lay through craggy rocks, shelving away unseen on one hand, and rising steeply against the burning sky on the other. We mounted steadily and slowly. I did not look much at Frank, but my eye was conscious of his figure, striding leisurely along. Now and then, when I turned to glance behind, I saw our shadows there diagonally on the road, and again I did not care for his hat. I had not seen him in a straw hat till that morning. We arrived at a second set of French custom-houses, deserted, and then we saw that the gigantic side of the mountain was cleft by a fissure from base to summit. And across the gorge had been thrown a tiny stone bridge to carry the road. At this point, by the bridge, the face of the rock had been carved smooth, and a great black triangle painted on it. And on the road was a common milestone, with 'France' on one side and 'Italia' on the other. And a very old man was harmlessly spreading a stock of picture postcards on the parapet of the bridge. My heart went out to that poor old man, whose white curls glinted in the sunlight. It seemed to me so pathetic that he should be just there, at that natural spot which the passions and the blood of men long dead had made artificial, tediously selling postcards in order to keep his worn and creaking body out of the grave.

'Do give him something,' I entreated Frank.

ARNOLD BENNETT

And while Frank went to him I leaned over the other parapet and listened for the delicate murmur of the stream far below. The split flank of the hill was covered with a large red blossom, and at the base, on the edge of the sea, were dolls' houses, each raising a slanted pencil of pale smoke.

Then we were in Italy, and still climbing. We saw a row of narrow, slattern cottages, their backs over the sea, and in front of them marched to and fro a magnificent soldier laced in gold, with chinking spurs and a rifle. Suddenly there ran out of a cottage two little girls, aged about four years and eight years, dirty, unkempt, delicious, shrill, their movements full of the ravishing grace of infancy. They attacked the laced soldier, chattering furiously, grumbling at him, intimidating him with the charming gestures of spoilt and pouting children. And he bent down stiffly in his superb uniform, and managed his long, heavy gun, and talked to them in a deep, vibrating voice. He reasoned with them till we could hear him no more. It was so touching, so exquisitely human!

We reached the top of the hill, having passed the Italian customs, equally vile with the French. The terraced grounds of an immense deserted castle came down to the roadside; and over the wall, escaped from the garden, there bloomed extravagantly a tangle of luscious yellow roses, just out of our reach. The road was still and deserted. We could see nothing but the road and the sea and the hills, all steeped, bewitched, and glorious under the sun. The ship had nearly slid to Mentone. The curving coastline of Italy wavered away into the shimmering horizon. And there were those huge roses, insolently blooming in the middle of winter, the symbol of the terrific forces of nature which slept quiescent under the universal calm. Perched as it were in a niche of the hills, we were part of that tremendous and ennobling scene. Long since the awkward self-consciousness caused by our plight had left us. We did not use speech, but we knew that we thought alike, and were suffering the same transcendent emotion. Was it joy or sadness? Rather than either, it was an admixture of both, originating in a poignant sense of the grandeur of life and of the earth.

'Oh, Frank,' I murmured, my spirit bursting, 'how beautiful it is!'

Our eyes met. He took me and kissed me impetuously, as though my utterance had broken a spell which enchained him. And as I kissed him I wept, blissfully. Nature had triumphed.

VI

We departed from Mentone that same day after lunch. I could not remove to his hotel; he could not remove to mine, for this was Mentone. We went to Monte Carlo by road, our luggage following. We chose Monte Carlo partly because it was the nearest place, and partly because it has some of the qualities—incurious, tolerant, unprovincial—of a capital city. If we encountered friends there, so much the better, in the end. The great adventure, the solemn and perilous enterprise had begun. I sent Yvonne for a holiday to her home in Laroche. Why? Ah, why? Perhaps for the simple reason that I had not the full courage of my convictions. We seldom have—*nous autres*. I felt that, if she had remained, Yvonne would have been too near me in the enterprise. I could not at first have been my natural self with her. I told the astonished and dissatisfied Yvonne that I would write to her as soon as I wanted her. Yet in other ways I had courage, and I found a delicious pleasure in my courage. When I was finally leaving the hotel I had Frank by my side. I behaved to him as to a husband. I publicly called him 'dear.' I asked his advice in trifles. He paid my bill. He even provided the money necessary for Yvonne. My joy in the possession of this male creature, whose part it now was to do for me a thousand things that hitherto I had been forced to do for myself, was almost naive. I could not hide it. I was at last a man's woman. I had a protector. Yes; I must not shrink from the equivocal significance of that word—I had a protector.

Frank was able to get three rooms at the Hotel de Paris at Monte Carlo. I had only to approve them. We met in our sitting-room at half-past three, ready to go out for a walk. It would be inexact to say that we were not nervous. But we were happy. He had not abandoned his straw hat.

'Don't wear that any more,' I said to him, smiling.

'But why? It's quite new.'

'It doesn't suit you,' I said.

'Oh, that doesn't matter,' he laughed, and he put it on.

'But I don't like to see you in it,' I persisted.

'Well, you'll stand it this afternoon, my angel, and I'll get another to-morrow.'

'Haven't you got another one here?' I asked, with discontent.

'No,' and he laughed again.

'But, dear—' I pouted.

He seemed suddenly to realize that as a fact I did not like the hat.

'Come here,' he said, charmingly grave; and he led me by the hand into his bedroom, which was littered with clothes, small parcels, boots, and brushes. One chair was overturned.

'Heavens!' I muttered, pretending to be shocked at the disorder.

He drew, me to a leather box of medium size.

'You can open it,' he said.

I opened it. The thing was rather a good contrivance, for a man. It held a silk hat, an opera hat, a bowler hat, some caps, and a soft Panama straw.

'And you said you had no others!' I grumbled at him.

'Well, which is it to be?' he demanded.

'This, of course,' I said, taking the bowler. I reached up, removed the straw hat from his head, and put the bowler in its place. 'There!' I exclaimed, satisfied, giving the bowler a pat—there!'

He laughed, immensely content, enraptured, foolishly blissful. We were indeed happy. Before opening the door leading to the corridor we stopped and kissed.

On the seaward terrace of the vast, pale, floriated Casino, so impressive in its glittering vulgarity, like the bride-cake of a stockbroker's wedding, we strolled about among a multifarious crowd, immersed in ourselves. We shared a contempt for the architecture, the glaring flower-beds, and the false distinction of the crowd, and an enthusiasm for the sunshine and the hills and the sea, and whatever else had escaped the hands of the Casino administration. We talked lightly and freely. Care seemed to be leaving us; we had no preoccupations save those which were connected with our passion. Then I saw, standing in an attitude of attention, the famous body-servant of Lord Francis Alcar, and I knew that Lord Francis could not be far away. We spoke to the valet; he pointed out his master, seated at the front of the terrace, and told us, in a discreet, pained, respectful voice, that our venerable friend had been mysteriously unwell at Monte Carlo, and was now taking the air for the first time in ten days. I determined that we should go boldly and speak to him.

'Lord Francis,' I said gently, after we had stood some seconds by his chair, unremarked.

He was staring fixedly at the distance of the sea. He looked amazingly older than when I had last talked with him. His figure was shrunken, and his face rose thin and white out of a heavy fur overcoat and a large blue muffler. In his eyes there was such a sadness, such an infinite regret, such a profound weariness as can only be seen in the eyes of the senile. He was utterly changed.

'Lord Francis,' I repeated, 'don't you know me?'

He started slightly and looked at me, and a faint gleam appeared in his eyes. Then he nodded, and took a thin, fragile alabaster hand out of the pocket of his overcoat. I shook it. It was like shaking hands with a dead, starved child. He carefully moved the skin and bone back into his pocket.

'Are you pretty well?' I said.

He nodded. Then the faint gleam faded out of his eyes; his head fell a little, and he resumed his tragic contemplation of the sea. The fact of my presence had dropped like a pebble into the strange depths of that aged mind, and the waters of the ferocious egotism of senility had closed over it, and it was forgotten. His rapt and yet meaningless gaze frightened me. It was as if there was more desolation and disillusion in that gaze than I had previously imagined the whole earth to contain. Useless for Frank to rouse him for the second time. Useless to explain ourselves. What was love to him, or the trivial conventions of a world which he was already quitting?

We walked away. From the edge of the terrace I could see a number of boats pulling to and fro in the water.

'It's the pigeon-shooting,' Frank explained. 'Come to the railings and you'll be able to see.'

I had already heard the sharp popping of rifles. I went to the railings, and saw a number of boxes arranged in a semicircle on a green, which was, as it were, suspended between the height of the terrace and the sea. Suddenly one of the boxes collapsed with a rattle, and a bird flew out of the ruin of it. There were two reports of a gun; the bird, its curving flight cut short, fell fluttering to the grass; a dog trotted out from the direction of the gun unseen beneath us, and disappeared again with the mass of ruffled feathers in its mouth. Then two men showed themselves, ran to the collapsed box, restored it, and put in it a fresh victim, and disappeared after the dog. I was horrified, but I could not remove my eyes from the green. Another box fell flat, and another bird flew out; a gun sounded; the bird soared far away, wavered, and sank on to the surface of the sea, and the boats converged towards it in furious haste. So the game proceeded. I saw a dozen deaths on the green; a few birds fell into the sea, and one escaped, settling ultimately on the roof of the Casino.

'So that is pigeon-shooting,' I said coldly, turning to Frank. 'I suppose it goes on all day?'

He nodded.

'It's just as cruel as plenty of other sports, and no more,' he said, as if apologizing for the entire male sex.

'I presume so,' I answered. 'But do you know, dear, if the idea once gets into my head that that is going on all day, I shan't be able to stop here. Let us have tea somewhere.'

Not until dinner did I recover from the obsession of that continual slaughter and destruction of beautiful life. It seemed to me that the Casino and its gorgeous gardens were veritably established on the mysterious arched hollow, within the high cliff, from which death shot out all day and every day. But I did recover perfectly. Only now do I completely perceive how violent, how capricious and contradictory were my emotions in those unique and unforgettable hours.

We dined late, because I had deprived myself of Yvonne. Already I was almost in a mind to send for her. The restaurant of the hotel was full, but we recognised no one as we walked through the room to our table.

'There is one advantage in travelling about with you,' said Frank.

'What is it?' I asked.

'No matter where one is, one can always be sure of being with the most beautiful woman in the place.'

I was content. I repaid him by being more than ever a man's woman. I knew that I was made for that. I understood why great sopranos have of their own accord given up even the stage on marriage. The career of literature seemed to me tedious and sordid in comparison with that of being a man's woman. In my rich black dress and my rings and bracelets I felt like an Eastern Empress; I felt that I could adequately reward homage with smiles, and love with fervid love. And I felt like a cat—idle, indolently graceful, voluptuously seeking warmth and caresses. I enveloped Frank with soft glances, I dazed him with glances. He ordered a wine which he said was fit for gods, and the waiter brought it reverently and filled our glasses, with a ritual of precautions. Later during the dinner Frank asked me if I would prefer champagne. I said, 'No, of course not.' But he said, 'I think you would,' and ordered some. 'Admit,' he said, 'that you prefer champagne.' 'Well, of course,' I replied. But I drank very little champagne, lest I should be too happy. Frank's wonderful face grew delicately flushed. The room resounded with discreet chatter, and the tinkle of glass and silver and porcelain. The upper part of it remained in shadow, but every table was a centre of rosy light, illuminating faces and jewels and napery. And in my sweet illusion I thought that every face had found the secret of joy, and that even the old had preserved it. Pleasure reigned. Pleasure was the sole goddess. And how satisfying then was the worship of her! Life had no inconveniences, no dark spots, no pitfalls. The gratification of the senses, the appeasing of appetites that instantly renewed themselves—this was the business of the soul. And as the wine sank lower in the bottles, and we cooled our tongues with ices, and the room began to empty, expectation gleamed and glittered in our eyes. At last, except a group of men smoking and talking in a corner, we were the only diners left.

'Shall we go?' Frank said, putting a veil of cigarette smoke between us.

I trembled. I was once more the young and timid girl. I could not speak. I nodded.

In the hall was Vicary, talking to the head-porter. He saw us and started.

'What! Vicary!' I murmured, suddenly cooled.

'I want to speak to you,' said Vicary. 'Where can we go?'

'This way,' Frank replied.

We went to our sitting-room, silent and apprehensive.

'Sit down,' said Vicary, shutting the door and standing against it.

He was wearing a tourist suit, with a gray overcoat, and his grizzled hair was tumbling over his hard, white face.

'What's the matter?' Frank asked. 'Anything wrong?'

'Look here, you two,' said Vicary, 'I don't want to discuss your position, and I'm the last person in this world to cast the first stone; but it falls to me to do it. I was coming down to Nice to stay with my sisters, and I've come a little further. My sisters wired me they had seen you. I've been to Mentone, and driven here from there. I hoped I should get here earlier than the newspapers, and I have done, it seems.'

'Earlier than the newspapers?' Frank repeated, standing up.

'Try to keep calm,' Vicary continued. 'Your wife's body was found in the Thames at seven o'clock last night. The doctors say it had been in the water for forty-eight hours. Your servants thought she had gone to you. But doubtless some thoughtful person had told her that you two were wandering about Europe together.'

'*My wife*' cried Frank.

And the strange and terrible emphasis he put on the word 'wife' proved to me in the fraction of a second that in his heart I was not his wife. A fearful tragedy had swept away the structure of argument in favour of the rights of love which he had built over the original conventionality of his mind. Poor fellow!

He fell back into his chair and covered his eyes.

'I thank God my mother didn't live to see this!' he cried.

And then he rushed to his bedroom and banged the door.

'My poor girl!' said Vicary, approaching me. 'What can I—I'm awfully—'

I waved him away.

'What's that?' he exclaimed, in a different voice, listening.

I ran to the bedroom, and saw Frank lifting a revolver.

'You've brought me to this, Carlotta!' he shouted.

I sprang towards him, but it was too late.

PART III

THE VICTORY

SACRED AND PROFANE LOVE

I

When I came out of the house, hurried and angrily flushing, I perceived clearly that my reluctance to break a habit and my desire for physical comfort, if not my attachment to the girl, had led me too far. I was conscious of humiliation. I despised myself. The fact was that I had quarrelled with Yvonne—Yvonne, who had been with me for eight years, Yvonne who had remained sturdily faithful during my long exile. Now the woman who quarrels with a maid is clumsy, and the woman who quarrels with a good maid is either a fool or in a nervous, hysterical condition, or both. Possibly I was both. I had permitted Yvonne too much liberty. I had spoilt her. She was fidelity itself, goodness itself; but her character had not borne the strain of realizing that she had acquired power over me, and that she had become necessary to me. So that morning we had differed violently; we had quarrelled as equals. The worst side of her had appeared suddenly, shockingly. And she had left me, demonstrating even as she banged the door that she was at least my mistress in altercation. All day I fought against the temptation to eat my pride, and ask her to return. It was a horrible, a deplorable, temptation. And towards evening, after seven hours of solitude in the hotel in the Avenue de Kleber, I yielded to it. I knew the address to which she had gone, and I took a cab and drove there, hating myself. I was received with excessive rudeness by a dirty and hag-like concierge, who, after refusing all information for some minutes, informed me at length that the young lady in question had quitted Paris in company with a gentleman.

The insolence of the concierge, my weakness and my failure, the bitter sense of lost dignity, the fact that Yvonne had not hesitated even a few hours before finally abandoning me—all these things wounded me. But the sharpest stab of all was that during our stay in Paris Yvonne must have had secret relations with a man. I had hidden nothing from her; she, however, had not reciprocated my candour. I had imagined that she lived only for me....

Well, the truth cannot be concealed that the years of wandering which had succeeded the fatal night at Monte Carlo had done little to improve me. What would you have? For months and months my ears rang with Frank's despairing shout: '*You've* brought me to this, Carlotta!' And the profound injustice of that cry tainted even the sad sweetness of my immense sorrow. To this day, whenever I hear it, as I do still, my inmost soul protests, and all the excuses which my love found for him seem inadequate and unconvincing. I was a broken creature. (How few know what it means to be broken—to sink under a tremendous and overwhelming calamity! And yet who but they can understandingly sympathize with the afflicted?) As for my friends, I did not give them the occasion to desert me; I deserted them. For the second time in my career I tore myself up by the roots. I lived the nomad's life, in the usual European haunts of the nomad. And in five years I did not make a single new friend, scarcely an acquaintance. I lived in myself and on myself, nursing grief, nursing a rancour against fate, nursing an involuntary shame.... You know, the scandal of which I had been the centre was appalling; it touched the extreme. It must have nearly killed the excellent Mrs. Sardis. I did not dare to produce another novel. But after a year or so I turned to poetry, and I must admit that my poetry was accepted. But it was not enough to prevent me from withering—from shrivelling. I lost ground, and I was still losing it. I was becoming sinister, warped, peculiar, capricious, unaccountable. I guessed it then; I see it clearly now.

The house of the odious concierge was in a small, shabby street off the Boulevard du Montparnasse. I looked in vain for a cab. Even on the wide, straight, gas-lit boulevard there was not a cab, and I wondered why I had been so foolish as to dismiss the one in which I had arrived. The great, glittering electric cars floated horizontally along in swift succession, but they meant nothing to me; I knew not whence they came nor whither they went. I doubt if I had ever been in a tram-car. Without a cab I was as helpless and as timid as a young girl, I who was thirty-one, and had travelled and lived and suffered! Never had I been alone in the streets of a large city at night. And the September night was sultry and forbidding. I was afraid—I was afraid of the men who passed me, staring at me. One man spoke to me, and I literally shook with fear as I hastened on. What would I have given to have had the once faithful Yvonne by my side! Presently I came to the crossing of the Boulevard Raspail, and this boulevard, equally long, uncharitable, and mournful with the other, endless, stretching to infinity, filled me with horror. Yes, with the horror of solitude in a vast city. Oh, you solitary, you who have felt that horror descending upon you, desolating, clutching, and chilling the heart, you will comprehend me!

At the corner, of the two boulevards was a glowing cafe, the Café du Dome, with a row of chairs and little tables in front of its windows. And at one of these little tables sat a man, gazing absently at a green glass in a white saucer. I had almost gone past him when some instinct prompted me to the bravery of looking at him again. He was a stoutish man, apparently aged about forty-five, very fair, with a puffed face and melancholy eyes. And then it was as though someone had shot me in the breast. It was as if I must fall down and die—as if the sensations which I experienced were too acute—too elemental for me to support. I have never borne a child, but I imagine that the woman who becomes a mother may feel as I felt then, staggered at hitherto unsuspected possibilities of sensation. I stopped. I clung to the nearest table. There was ice on my shuddering spine, and a dew on my forehead.

'Magda!' breathed the man.

He had raised his eyes to mine.

It was Diaz, after ten years.

At first I had not recognised him. Instead of ten, he seemed twenty years older. I searched in his features for the man I had known, as the returned traveller searches the scene of his childhood for remembered landmarks. Yes, it was Diaz, though time had laid a heavy hand on him. The magic of his eyes was not effaced, and when he smiled youth reappeared.

'It is I,' I murmured.

He got up, and in doing so shook the table, and his glass was overturned, and scattered itself in fragments on the asphalte. At the noise a waiter ran out of the cafe, and Diaz, blushing and obviously making a great effort at self-control, gave him an order.

'I should have known you anywhere,' said Diaz to me, taking my hand, as the waiter went.

The ineptitude of the speech was such that I felt keenly sorry for him. I was not in the least hurt. My sympathy enveloped him. The position was so difficult, and he had seemed so pathetic, sitting there alone on the pavement of the vast nocturnal boulevard, so weighed down by sadness, that I wanted to comfort him and soothe him, and to restore him to all the brilliancy of his first period. It appeared to me unjust and cruel that the wheels of life should have crushed him too. And so I said, smiling as well as I could:

'And I you.'

'Won't you sit down here?' he suggested, avoiding my eyes.

And thus I found myself seated outside a cafe, at night, conspicuous for all Montparnasse to see. We never know what may lie in store for us at the next turning of existence.

'Then I am not much changed, you think?' he ventured, in an anxious tone.

'No,' I lied. 'You are perhaps a little stouter. That's all.'

How hard it was to talk! How lamentably self-conscious we were! How unequal to the situation! We did not know what to say.

'You are far more beautiful than ever you were,' he said, looking at me for an instant. 'You are a woman; you were a girl—then.'

The waiter brought another glass and saucer, and a second waiter followed him with a bottle, from which he poured a greenish-yellow liquid into the glass.

'What will you have?' Diaz asked me.

'Nothing, thank you,' I said quickly.

To sit outside the cafe was already much. It would have been impossible for me to drink there.

'Ah! as you please, as you please,' Diaz snapped. 'I beg your pardon.'

'Poor fellow!' I reflected. 'He must be suffering from nervous irritability.' And aloud, 'I'm not thirsty, thank you,' as nicely as possible.

He smiled beautifully; the irritability had passed.

'It's awfully kind of you to sit down here with me,' he said, in a lower voice. 'I suppose you've heard about me?'

He drank half the contents of the glass.

'I read in the papers some years ago that you were suffering from neurasthenia and nervous breakdown,' I replied. 'I was very sorry.'

'Yes,' he said; 'nervous breakdown—nervous breakdown.'

'You haven't been playing lately, have you?'

'It is more than two years since I played. And if you had heard me that time! My God!'

'But surely you have tried some cure?'

'Cure!' he repeated after me. 'There's no cure. Here I am! Me!'

His glass was empty. He tapped on the window behind us, and the procession of waiters occurred again, and Diaz received a third glass, which now stood on three saucers.

'You'll excuse me,' he said, sipping slowly. 'I'm not very well to-night. And you've—Why did you run away from me? I wanted to find you, but I couldn't.'

'Please do not let us talk about that,' I stopped him. 'I—I must go.'

'Oh, of course, if I've offended you—'

'No,' I said; 'I'm not at all offended. But I think—'

'Then, if you aren't offended, stop a little, and let me see you home. You're sure you won't have anything?'

I shook my head, wishing that he would not drink so much. I thought it could not be good for his nerves.

'Been in Paris long?' he asked me, with a slightly confused utterance.

'Staying in this quarter? Many English and Americans here.'

Then, in setting down the glass, he upset it, and it smashed on the pavement like the first one.

'Damn!' he exclaimed, staring forlornly at the broken glass, as if in the presence of some irreparable misfortune. And before I could put in a word, he turned to me with a silly smile, and approaching his face to mine till his hat touched the brim of my hat, he said thickly: 'After all, you know, I'm the greatish pianist in the world.'

The truth struck me like a blow. In my amazing ignorance of certain aspects of life I had not suspected it. Diaz was drunk. The ignominy of it! The tragedy of it! He was drunk. He had fallen to the beast. I drew back from that hot, reeking face.

'You don't think I am?' he muttered. 'You think young What's-his-name can play Ch—Chopin better than me? Is that it?'

I wanted to run away, to cease to exist, to hide with my shame in some deep abyss. And there I was on the boulevard, next to this animal, sharing his table and the degradation! And I could not move. There are people so gifted that in a dilemma they always know exactly the wisest course to adopt. But I did not know. This part of my story gives me infinite pain to write, and yet I must write it, though I cannot persuade myself to write it in full; the details would be too repulsive. Nevertheless, forget not that I lived it.

He put his face to mine again, and began to stammer something, and I drew away.

'You are ashamed of me, madam,' he said sharply.

'I think you are not quite yourself—not quite well,' I replied.

'You mean I am drunk.'

'I mean what I say. You are not quite well. Please do not twist my words.'

'You mean I am drunk,' he insisted, raising his voice. 'I am not drunk; I have never been drunk. That I can swear with my hand on my heart. But you are ashamed of being seen with me.'

'I think you ought to go home,' I suggested.

'That is only to get rid of me!' he cried.

'No, no,' I appealed to him persuasively. 'Do not wound me. I will go with you as far as your house, if you like. You are too ill to be alone.'

At that moment an empty open cab strolled by, and, without pausing for his answer, I signalled the driver. My heart beat wildly. My spirit was in an uproar. But I was determined not to desert him, not to abandon him to a public disgrace. I rose from my seat.

'You're very good,' he said, in a new voice.

The cab had stopped.

'Come!' I entreated him.

He rapped uncertainly on the window, and then, as the waiter did not immediately appear, he threw some silver on the table, and aimed himself in the direction of the cab. I got in. Diaz slipped on the step.

'I've forgotten somethin',' he complained. 'What is it? My umbrella—yes, my umbrella—*pépina*s they say here. 'Scuse me moment.'

His umbrella was, in fact, lying under a chair. He stooped with difficulty and regained it, and then the waiter, who had at length arrived, helped him into the cab, and he sank like a mass of inert clay on my skirts.

'Tell the driver the address,' I whispered.

The driver, with head turned and a grin on his face, was waiting.

'Rue de Douai,' said Diaz sullenly.

'What number?' the driver asked.

'Does that regard you?' Diaz retorted crossly in French. 'I will tell you later.'

'Tell him now,' I pleaded.

'Well, to oblige you, I will. Twenty-seven. But what I can't stand is the impudence of these fellows.'

The driver winked at me.

'Just so,' I soothed Diaz, and we drove off.

I have never been happier than in unhappiness. Happiness is not joy, and it is not tranquillity. It is something deeper and something more disturbing. Perhaps it is an acute sense of life, a realization of one's secret being, a continual renewal of the mysterious savour of existence. As I crossed Paris with the drunken Diaz leaning clumsily against my shoulder, I was profoundly unhappy. I was desolated by the sight of this ruin, and yet I was happier than I had been since Frank died. I had glimpses and intimations of the baffling essence of our human lives here, strange, fleeting comprehensions of the eternal wonder and the eternal beauty.... In vain, professional writer as I am, do I try to express myself. What I want to say cannot be said; but those who have truly lived will understand.

We passed over the Seine, lighted and asleep in the exquisite Parisian night, and the rattling of the cab on the cobble-stones roused Diaz from his stupor.

'Where are we?' he asked.

'Just going through the Louvre,' I replied.

'I don't know how I got to the other s-side of the river,' he said. 'Don't remember. So you're coming home with me, eh? You aren't 'shamed of me?'

'You are hurting me,' I said coldly, 'with your elbow.'

'Oh, a thousand pardons! a thous' parnds, Magda! That isn't your real name, is it?'

He sat upright and turned his face to glance at mine with a fatuous smile; but I would not look at him. I kept my eyes straight in front. Then a swerve of the carriage swung his body away from me, and he subsided into the corner. The intoxication was gaining on him every minute.

'What shall I do with him?' I thought.

I blushed as we drove up the Avenue de l'Opera and across the Grand Boulevard, for it seemed to me that all the gay loungers must observe Diaz' condition. We followed darker thoroughfares, and at last the cab, after climbing a hill, stopped before a house in a street that appeared rather untidy and irregular. I got out first, and Diaz stumbled after me, while two women on the opposite side of the road stayed curiously to watch us. Hastily I opened my purse and gave the driver a five-franc-piece, and he departed before Diaz could decide what to say. I had told him to go.

I did not wish to tell the driver to go. I told him in spite of myself.

Diaz, grumbling inarticulately, pulled the bell of the great door of the house. But he had to ring several times before finally the door opened; and each second was a year for me, waiting there with him in the street. And when the door opened he was leaning against it, and so pitched forward into the gloom of the archway. A laugh—the loud, unrestrained laugh of the courtesan—came from across the street.

The archway was as black as night.

'Shut the door, will you?' I heard Diaz' voice. 'I can't see it.

Where are you?'

But I was not going to shut the door.

'Have you got a servant here?' I asked him.

'She comes in the mornings,' he replied.

'Then there is no one in your flat?'

'Not a shoul,' said Diaz. 'Needn't be 'fraid.'

I'm not afraid,' I said. 'But I wanted to know. Which floor is it?'

'Third. I'll light a match.'

Then I pushed to the door, whose automatic latch clicked. We were fast in the courtyard.

Diaz dropped his matches in attempting to strike one. The metal box bounced on the tiles. I bent down and groped with both hands till I found it. And presently we began painfully to ascend the staircase, Diaz holding his umbrella and the rail, and I striking matches from time to time. We were on the second landing when I heard the bell ring again, and the banging of the front-door, and then voices at the foot of the staircase. I trembled lest we should be over-taken, and I would have hurried Diaz on, but he would not be hurried. Happily, as we were halfway between the second and third story, the man and the girl whose voices I heard stopped at the second. I caught sight of them momentarily through the banisters. The man was striking matches as I had been. '*C'est ici,*' the girl whispered. She was dressed in blue with a very large hat. She put a key in the door when they had stopped, and then our matches went out simultaneously. The door shut, and Diaz and I were alone on the staircase again. I struck another match; we struggled on.

When I had taken his key from Diaz' helpless hand, and opened his door and guided him within, and closed the door definitely upon the outer world, I breathed a great sigh. Every turn of the stair had been a station of the cross for me. We were now in utter darkness. The classical effluvium of inebriety mingled with the classical odour of the furnished lodging. But I cared not. I had at last successfully hidden his shame. No one could witness it now but me. So I was glad.

Neither of us said anything as, still with the aid of matches, I penetrated into the flat. Silently I peered about until I perceived a pair of candles, which I lighted. Diaz, with his hat on his head and his umbrella clasped tightly in his hand, fell into a chair. We glanced at each other.

'You had better go to bed,' I suggested. 'Take your hat off. You will feel better without it.'

He did not move, and I approached him and gently took his hat. I then touched the umbrella.

'No, no, no!' he cried suddenly; 'I'm always losing this umbrella, and I won't let it out of my sight.'

'As you wish,' I replied coldly.

I was standing by him when he got up with a surprising lurch and put a hand on my shoulder. He evidently meant to kiss me. I kept him at arm's length, feeling a sort of icy anger.

'Go to bed,' I repeated fiercely. 'It is the only place for you.'

He made inarticulate noises in his throat, and ultimately achieved the remark:

'You're very hard, Magda.'

Then he bent himself towards the next room.

'You will want a candle,' I said, with bitterness. 'No; I will carry it.

Let me go first.'

I preceded him through a tiny salon into the bedroom, and, leaving him there with one candle, came back into the first room. The whole place was deplorable, though not more deplorable than I had expected from the look of the street and the house and the stairs and the girl with the large hat. It was small, badly arranged, disordered, ugly, bare, comfortless, and, if not very dirty, certainly not clean; not a home, but a kennel—a kennel furnished with chairs and spotted mirrors and spotted engravings and a small upright piano; a kennel whose sides were covered with enormous red poppies, and on whose floor was something which had once been a carpet; a kennel fitted with windows and curtains; a kennel with actually a bed! It was the ready-made human kennel of commerce, which every large city supplies wholesale in tens of thousands to its victims. In that street there were hundreds such; in the house alone there were probably a score at least. Their sole virtue was their privacy. Ah the blessedness of the sacred outer door, which not even the tyrant concierge might violate! I thought of all the other interiors of the house, floor above floor, and serried one against another—vile, mean, squalid, cramped, unlovely, frowsy, fetid; but each lighted and intensely alive with the interplay of hearts; each cloistered, a secure ground where the instincts that move the world might show themselves naturally and in secret. There was something tragically beautiful in that.

I had heard uncomfortable sounds from the bedroom. Then Diaz called out:

'It's no use. Can't do it. Can't get into bed.' I went directly to him.

He sat on the bed, still clasping the umbrella, one arm out of his coat.

His gloomy and discouraged face was the face of a man who retires baffled

from some tremendously complicated problem.

'Put down your umbrella,' I said. 'Don't be foolish.'

'I'm not foolish,' he retorted irritably. 'Don't want to loosh thish umbrella again.'

'Well then,' I said, 'hold it in the other hand, and I will help you.'

This struck him as a marvellous idea, one of those discoveries that revolutionize science, and he instantly obeyed. He was now very drunk. He was nauseating. The conventions which society has built up in fifty centuries ceased suddenly to exist. It was impossible that they should exist—there in that cabin, where we were alone together, screened, shut in. I lost even the sense of convention. I was no longer disgusted. Everything that was seemed natural, ordinary, normal. I became his mother. I became his hospital nurse. And at length he lay in bed, clutching the umbrella to his breast. Nothing had induced him to loose it from both hands at once. The priceless value of the umbrella was the one clearly-defined notion that illuminated his poor devastated brain. I left him to his inanimate companion.

II

I should have left then, though I had a wish not to leave. But I was prevented from going by the fear of descending those sinister stairs alone, and the necessity of calling aloud to the concierge in order to get out through the main door, and the possible difficulties in finding a cab in that region at that hour. I knew that I could not have borne to walk even to the end of the street unprotected. So I stayed where I was, seated in a chair near the window of the larger room, saturating myself in the vague and heavy flood of sadness that enwraps the fretful, passionate city in the night—the night when the commonest noises seem to carry some mystic message to the listening soul, the night when truth walks abroad naked and whispers her secrets.

A gas-lamp threw its radiance on the ceiling in bars through the slits of the window-shutters, and then, far in the middle wilderness of the night, the lamp was extinguished by a careful municipality, and I was left in utter darkness. Long since the candles had burnt away. I grew silly and sentimental, and pictured the city in feverish sleep, gaining with difficulty inadequate strength for the morrow—as if the city had not been living this life for centuries and did not know exactly what it was about! And then, sure as I had been that I could not sleep, I woke up, and I could see the outline of the piano. Dawn had begun. And not a sound disturbed the street, and not a sound came from Diaz' bedroom. As of old, he slept with the tranquillity of a child.

And after a time I could see the dust on the piano and on the polished floor under the table. The night had passed, and it appeared to be almost a miracle that the night had passed, and that I had lived through it and was much the same Carlotta still. I gently opened the window and pushed back the shutters. A young woman, tall, with a superb bust, clothed in blue, was sweeping the footpath in long, dignified strokes of a broom. She went slowly from my ken. Nothing could have been more prosaic, more sane, more astringent. And yet only a few hours—and it had been night, strange, voluptuous night! And even now a thousand thousand pillows were warm and crushed under their burden of unconscious dreaming souls. But that tall woman must go to bed in day, and rise to meet the first wind of the morning, and perhaps never have known the sweet poison of the night. I sank back into my chair....

There was a sharp, decisive sound of a key in the lock of the entrance-door. I jumped up, fully awake, with beating heart and blushing face. Someone was invading the flat. Someone would catch me there.

Of course it was his servant. I had entirely forgotten her.

We met in the little passage. She was a stout creature and appeared to fill the flat. She did not seem very surprised at the sight of me, and she eyed me with the frigid disdain of one who conforms to a certain code for one who does not conform to it. She sat in judgment on my well-hung skirt and the rings on my fingers and the wickedness in my breast, and condemned me to everlasting obloquy.

'Madame is going?' she asked coldly, holding open the door.

'No, madame,' I said. 'Are you the *femme de ménage* of monsieur?'

'Yes, madame.'

'Monsieur is ill,' I said, deciding swiftly what to do. 'He does not wish to be disturbed. He would like you to return at two o'clock.'

Long before two I should have departed.

'Monsieur knows well that I have another *ménage* from twelve to two,' protested the woman.

'Three o'clock, then,' I said.

Bien, madame,' said she, and, producing the contents of a reticule: 'Here are the bread, the butter, the milk, and the newspaper, madame.'

'Thank you, madame.'

I took the things, and she left, and I shut the door and bolted it.

In anticipation, the circumstances of such an encounter would have caused me infinite trouble of spirit. 'But after all it was not so very dreadful,' I thought, as I fastened the door. 'Do I care for his *femme de ménage*?'

The great door of the house would be open now, and the stairs no longer affrighting, and I might slip unobserved away. But I could not bring myself to leave until I had spoken with Diaz, and I would not wake him. It was nearly noon when he stirred. I heard his movements, and a slight moaning sigh, and he called me.

'Are you there, Magda?'

How feeble and appealing his voice!

For answer I stepped into his bedroom.

The eye that has learned to look life full in the face without a quiver of the lid should find nothing repulsive. Everything that is is the ordered and calculable result of environment. Nothing can be abhorrent, nothing blameworthy, nothing contrary to nature. Can we exceed nature? In the presence of the primeval and ever-continuing forces of nature, can we maintain our fantastic conceptions of sin and of justice? We are, and that is all we should dare to say. And yet, when I saw Diaz stretched on that wretched bed my first movement was one of physical disgust. He had not shaved for several days. His hair was like a doormat. His face was unclean and puffed; his lips full and cracked; his eyes all discoloured. If aught can be vile, he was vile. If aught can be obscene, he was obscene. His limbs twitched; his features were full of woe and desolation and abasement.

He looked at me heavily, mournfully.

'Diaz, Diaz!' said my soul. 'Have you come to this?'

A great and overmastering pity seized me, and I went to him, and laid my hand gently on his. He was so nervous and tremulous that he drew away his hand as if I had burnt it.

'Oh, Magda,' he murmured, 'my head! There was a piece of hot brick in my mouth, and I tried to take it out. But it was my tongue. Can I have some tea? Will you give me some cold water first?'

Strange that the frank and simple way in which he accepted my presence there, and assumed my willingness to serve him, filled me with a new joy! He said nothing of the night. I think that Diaz was one of the few men who are strong enough never to regret the past. If he was melancholy, it was merely because he suffered bodily in the present.

I gave him water, and he thanked me.

'Now I will make some tea,' I said.

And I went into the tiny kitchen and looked around, lifting my skirts.

'Can you find the things?' he called out.

'Yes,' I said.

'What's all that splashing?' he inquired.

'I'm washing a saucepan,' I said.

'I never have my meals here,' he called. 'Only tea. There are two taps to the gas-stove—one a little way up the chimney.'

Yes, I was joyous, actively so. I brought the tea to the bedroom with a glad smile. I had put two cups on the tray, which I placed on the night-table; and there were some biscuits. I sat at the foot of the bed while we drank. And the umbrella, unperceived by Diaz, lay with its handle on a pillow, ludicrous and yet accusing.

'You are an angel,' said Diaz.

'Don't call me that,' I protested.

'Why not?'

'Because I wish it,' I said. 'Angel' was Ispenlove's word.

'Then, what shall I call you?'

'My name is Carlotta Peel,' I said. 'Not Magdalen at all.'

It was astounding, incredible, that he should be learning my name then for the first time.

'I shall always call you Magda,' he responded.

'And now I must go,' I stated, when I had explained to him about the servant.

'But you'll come back?' he cried.

No question of his coming to me! I must come to him!

'To a place like this?' I demanded.

Unthinkingly I put into my voice some of the distaste I felt for his deplorable apartments, and he was genuinely hurt. I believe that in all honesty he deemed his apartments to be quite adequate and befitting. His sensibilities had been so dulled.

He threw up his head.

'Of course,' he said, 'if you—'

'No, no!' I stopped him quickly. 'I will come here. I was only teasing you. Let me see. I'll come back at four, just to see how you are. Won't you get up in the meantime?'

He smiled, placated.

'I may do,' he said. 'I'll try to. But in case I don't, will you take my key? Where did you put it last night?'

'I have it,' I said.

He summoned me to him just as I was opening the door.

'Magda!'

'What is it?'

I returned.

'You are magnificent,' he replied, with charming, impulsive eagerness, his eyes resting upon me long. He was the old Diaz again. 'I can't thank you. But when you come back I shall play to you.'

I smiled.

'Till four o'clock,' I said.

'Magda,' he called again, just as I was leaving, 'bring one of your books with you, will you?'

I hesitated, with my hand on the door. When I gave him my name he had made no sign that it conveyed to him anything out of the ordinary. That was exactly like Diaz.

'Have you read any of them?' I asked loudly, without moving from the door.

'No,' he answered. 'But I have heard of them.'

'Really!' I said, keeping my tone free from irony. 'Well, I will not bring you one of my books.'

'Why not?'

I looked hard at the door in front of me.

'For you I will be nothing but a woman,' I said.

And I fled down the stairs and past the concierge swiftly into the street, as anxious as a thief to escape notice. I got a fiacre at once, and drove away. I would not analyze my heart. I could not. I could but savour the joy, sweet and fresh, that welled up in it as from some secret source. I was so excited that I observed nothing outside myself, and when the cab stopped in front of my hotel, it seemed to me that the journey had occupied scarcely a few seconds. Do you imagine I was saddened by the painful spectacle of Diaz' collapse in life? No! I only knew that he needed sympathy, and that I could give it to him with both hands. I could give, give! And the last thing that the egotist in me told me before it expired was that I was worthy to give. My longing to assuage the lot of Diaz became almost an anguish.

III

I returned at about half-past five, bright and eager, with vague anticipations. I seemed to have become used to the house. It no longer offended me, and I had no shame in entering it. I put the key into the door of Diaz' flat with a clear, high sense of pleasure. He had entrusted me with his key; I could go in as I pleased; I need have no fear of inconveniencing him, of coming at the wrong moment. It seemed wonderful! And as I turned the key and pushed open the door my sole wish was to be of service to him, to comfort him, to render his life less forlorn.

'Here I am!' I cried, shutting the door.

There was no answer.

In the smaller of the two tiny sitting-rooms the piano, which had been closed, was open, and I saw that it was a Pleyel. But both rooms were empty.

'Are you still in bed, then?' I said.

There was still no answer.

I went cautiously into the bedroom. It, too, was empty. The bed was made, and the flat generally had a superficial air of tidiness. Evidently the charwoman had been and departed; and doubtless Diaz had gone out, to return immediately. I sat down in the chair in which I had spent most of the night. I took off my hat and put it by the side of a tiny satchel which I had brought, and began to wait for him. How delicious it would be to open the door to him! He would notice that I had taken off my hat, and he would be glad. What did the future, the immediate future, hold for me?

A long time I waited, and then I yawned heavily, and remembered that for several days I had had scarcely any sleep. I shut my eyes to relieve the tedium of waiting. When I reopened them, dazed, and startled into sudden activity by mysterious angry noises, it was quite dark. I tried to recall where I was, and to decide what the noises could be. I regained my faculties with an effort. The noises were a beating on the door.

'It is Diaz,' I said to myself; 'and he can't get in!'

And I felt very guilty because I had slept. I must have slept for hours.

Groping for a candle, I lighted it.

'Coming! coming!' I called in a loud voice.

And I went into the passage with the candle and opened the door.

It was Diaz. The gas was lighted on the stairs. Between that and my candle he stood conspicuous in all his details. Swaying somewhat, he supported himself by the balustrade, and was thus distant about two feet from the door. He was drunk—viciously drunk; and in an instant I knew the cruel truth concerning him, and wondered that I had not perceived it before. He was a drunkard—simply that. He had not taken to drinking as a consequence of nervous breakdown. Nervous breakdown was a euphemism for the result of alcoholic excess. I saw his slow descent as in a vision, and everything was explained. My heart leapt.

'I can save him,' I said to myself. 'I can restore him.'

I was aware of the extreme difficulty of curing a drunkard, of the immense proportion of failures. But, I thought, if a woman such as I cannot by the lavishing of her whole soul and body deliver from no matter what fiend a man such as Diaz, then the world has changed, and the eternal Aphrodite is dead.

'I can save him!' I repeated.

Oh, heavenly moment!

'Aren't you coming in?' I addressed him quietly. 'I've been waiting for you.'

'Have you?' he angrily replied. 'I waited long enough for you.'

'Well,' I said, 'come in.'

'Who is it?' he demanded. 'I inzizt—who is it?'

'It's I,' I answered; 'Magda.'

'That's no' wha' I mean,' he went on. 'And wha's more—you know it. Who is it addrezzes you, madame?'

'Why,' I humoured him, 'it's you, of course—Diaz.'

There was the sound of a door opening on one of the lower storeys, and I hoped I had pacified him, and that he would enter; but I was mistaken. He stamped his foot furiously on the landing.

'Diaz!' he protested, shouting. 'Who dares call me Diaz? Wha's my full name?'

'Emilio Diaz,' I murmured meekly.

'That's better,' he grumbled. 'What am I?'

I hesitated.

'Wha' am I?' he roared; and his voice went up and down the echoing staircase. 'I won't put foot ev'n on doormat till I'm told wha' I am here.'

'You are the—the master,' I said. 'But do come in.'

'The mas'r! Mas'r of wha'?'

'Master of the pianoforte,' I answered at once.

He smiled, suddenly appeased, and put his foot unsteadily on the doormat.

'Good!' he said. 'But, un'stan', I wouldn't ev'n have pu' foot on doormat—no, not ev'n on doormat—'

And he came in, and I shut the door, and I was alone with my wild beast.

'Kiss me,' he commanded.

I kissed him on the mouth.

'You don't put your arms roun' me,' he growled.

So I deposited the candle on the floor, and put my arms round his neck, standing on tip-toe, and kissed him again.

He went past me, staggering and growling, into the sitting-room at the end of the passage, and furiously banged down the lid of the piano, so that every cord in it jangled deafeningly.

'Light the lamp,' he called out.

'In one second,' I said.

I locked the outer door on the inside, slipped the key into my pocket, and picked up the candle.

'What were you doing out there?' he demanded.

'Nothing,' I said. 'I had to pick the candle up.'

He seized my hat from the table and threw it to the floor. Then he sat down.

'Nex' time,' he remarked, 'you'll know better'n to keep me waiting.'

I lighted a lamp.

'I'm very sorry,' I said. 'Won't you go to bed?'

'I shall go to bed when I want,' he answered. 'I'm thirsty. In the cupboard you'll see a bottle. I'll trouble you to give it me, with a glass and some water.'

'This cupboard?' I said questioningly, opening a cupboard papered to match the rest of the wall.

'Yes.'

'But surely you can't be thirsty, Diaz?' I protested.

'Must I repea' wha' I said?' he glared at me. 'I'm thirsty. Give me the bottle.'

I took out the bottle nearest to hand. It was of a dark green colour, and labelled 'Extrait d'Absinthe. Pernod fils.'

'Not this one, Diaz?'

'Yes,' he insisted. 'Give it me. And get a glass and some water.'

'No,' I said firmly.

'Wha'? You won't give it me?'

'No.'

He jumped up recklessly and faced me. His hat fell off the back of his head.

'Give me that bottle!'

His breath poisoned the room.

I retreated in the direction of the window, and put my hand on the knob.

'No,' I said.

He sprang at me, but not before I had opened the window and thrown out the bottle. I heard it fall in the roadway with a crash and scattering of glass. Happily it had harmed no one. Diaz was momentarily checked.

He hesitated. I eyed him as steadily as I could, closing the while the window behind me with my right hand.

'He may try to kill me,' I thought.

My heart was thudding against my dress, not from fear, but from excitement. My situation seemed impossible to me, utterly passing belief. Yesterday I had been a staid spinster, attended by a maid, in a hotel of impeccable propriety. Today I had locked myself up alone with a riotous drunkard in a vile flat in a notorious Parisian street. Was I mad? What force, secret and powerful, had urged me on?... And there was the foul drunkard, with clenched hands and fiery eyes, undecided whether or not to murder me. And I waited.

He moved away, inarticulately grumbling, and resumed with difficulty his hat.

'Ver' well,' he hiccupped morosely, 'ver' well; I'm going. Tha's all.'

He lurched into the passage, and then I heard him fumbling a long time with the outer door. He left the door and went into his bedroom, and finally returned to me. He held one hand behind his back. I had sunk into a chair by the small table on which the lamp stood, with my satchel beside it.

'Now!' he said, halting in front of me. 'You've locked tha' door. I can't go out.'

'Yes,' I admitted.

'Give me the key.'

I shook my head.

'Give me the key,' he cried. 'I mus' have the key.'

I shook my head.

Then he showed his right hand, and it held a revolver. He bent slightly over the table, staring down at me as I stared up at him. But as his chin felt the heat rising from the chimney of the lamp, he shifted a little to one side. I might have rushed for shelter into some other room; I might have grappled with him; I might have attempted to soothe him. But I could neither stir nor speak. Least of all, could I give him the key—for him to go and publish his own disgrace in the thoroughfares. So I just gazed at him, inactive.

'I s'll kill you!' he muttered, and raised the revolver.

My throat became suddenly dry. I tried to make the motion of swallowing, and could not. And looking at the revolver, I perceived in a swift revelation the vast folly of my inexperience. Since he was already drunk, why had I not allowed him to drink more, to drink himself into a stupor? Drunkards can only be cured when they are sober. To commence a course of moral treatment at such a moment as I had chosen was indeed the act of a woman. However, it was too late to reclaim the bottle from the street.

I saw that he meant to kill me. And I knew that previously, during our encounter at the window, I had only pretended to myself that I thought there was a risk of his killing me. I had pretended, in order to increase the glory of my martyrdom in my own sight. Moreover, my brain, which was working with singular clearness, told me that for his sake I ought to give up the key. His exposure as a helpless drunkard would be infinitely preferable to his exposure as a murderer.

Yet I could not persuade myself to relinquish the key. If I did so, he would imagine that he had frightened me. But I had no fear, and I could not bear that he should think I had.

He fired.

My ears sang. The room was full of a new odour, and a cloud floated reluctantly upwards from the mouth of the revolver. I sneezed, and then I grew aware that, firing at a distant of two feet, he had missed me. What had happened to the bullet I could not guess. He put the revolver down on the table with a groan, and the handle rested on my satchel.

'My God, Magda!' he sighed, pushing back his hair with his beautiful hand.

He was somewhat sobered. I said nothing, but I observed that the lamp was smoking, and I turned down the wick. I was so self-conscious, so irresolute, so nonplussed, that in sheer awkwardness, like a girl at a party who does not know what to do with her hands, I pushed the revolver off the satchel, and idly unfastened the catch of the satchel. Within it, among other things, was my sedative. I, too, had fallen the victim of a habit. For five years a bad sleeper, I had latterly developed into a very bad sleeper, and my sedative was accordingly strong.

A notion struck me.

'Drink a little of this, my poor Diaz!' I murmured.

'What is it?' he asked.

'It will make you sleep,' I said.

With a convulsive movement he clutched the bottle and uncorked it, and before I could interfere he had drunk nearly the whole of its contents.

'Stop!' I cried. 'You will kill yourself!'

'What matter!' he exclaimed; and staggered off to the darkness of the bedroom.

I followed him with the lamp, but he had already fallen on the bed, and seemed to be heavily asleep. I shook him; he made no response.

'At any cost he must he roused,' I said aloud. 'He must be forced to walk.'

There was a knocking at the outer door, low, discreet, and continuous. It sounded to me like a deliverance. Whoever might be there must aid me to waken Diaz. I ran to the door, taking the key out of my pocket, and opened it. A tall woman stood on the doormat. It was the girl that I had glimpsed on the previous night in the large hat ascending the stairs with a man. But now her bright golden head was uncovered, and she wore a blue *peignoir*, such as is sold ready made, with its lace and its ribbons, at all the big Paris shops.

We both hesitated.

'Oh, pardon, madame,' she said, in a thin, sweet voice in French. 'I was at my door, and it seemed to me that I heard—a revolver. Nothing serious has passed, then? Pardon, madame.'

'Nothing, thank you. You are very amiable, madame,' I replied stiffly.

'All my excuses, madame,' said she, turning away.

'No, no!' I exclaimed. 'I am wrong. Do not go. Someone is ill—very ill.

If you would—'

She entered.

'Where? What is it?' she inquired.

'He is in the bedroom—here.'

We both spoke breathlessly, hurrying to the bedroom, after I had fetched the lamp.

'Wounded? He has done himself harm? Ah!'

'No,' I said, 'not that.'

And I explained to her that Diaz had taken at least six doses of my strong solution of trional.

I seized the lamp and held it aloft over the form of the sleeper, which lay on its side cross-wise, the feet projecting a little over the edge of the bed, the head bent forward and missing the pillow, the arms stretched out in front—the very figure of abandoned and perfect unconsciousness. And the girl and I stared at Diaz, our shoulders touching, in the kennel.

'He must be made to walk about,' I said. 'You would be extremely kind to help me.'

'No, madame,' she replied. 'He will be very well like that. When one is alcoholic, one cannot poison one's self; it is impossible. All the doctors will tell you as much. Your friend will sleep for twenty hours—twenty-four hours—and he will waken himself quite re-established.'

'You are sure? You know?'

'I know, madame. Be tranquil. Leave him. He could not have done better.

It is perfect.'

'Perhaps I should fetch a doctor?' I suggested.

'It is not worth the pain,' she said, with conviction. 'You would have vexations uselessly. Leave him.'

I gazed at her, studying her, and I was satisfied. With her fluffly locks, and her simple eyes, and her fragile face, and her long hands, she had, nevertheless, the air of knowing profoundly her subject. She was a great expert on males and all that appertained to them, especially their vices. I was the callow amateur. I was compelled to listen with respect to this professor in the professor's garb. I was impressed, in spite of myself.

'One might arrange him more comfortably,' she said.

And we lifted the senseless victim, and put him on his back, and straightened his limbs, as though he had been a corpse.

'How handsome he is!' murmured my visitor, half closing her eyes.

'You think so?' I said politely, as if she had been praising one of my private possessions.

'Oh yes. We are neighbours, madame. I have frequently remarked him, you understand, on the stairs, in the street.'

'Has he been here long?' I asked.

'About a year, madame. You have, perhaps, not seen him since a long time.

An old friend?'

'It is ten years ago,' I replied.

'Ah! Ten years! In England, without doubt?'

'In England, yes.'

'Ten years!' she repeated, musing.

'I am certain she has a kind heart,' I said to myself, and I decided to question her: 'Will you not sit down, madame?' I invited her.

'Ah, madame! it is you who should sit down,' she said quickly. 'You must have suffered.'

We both sat down. There were only two chairs in the room.

'I would like to ask you,' I said, leaning forward towards her, 'have you ever seen him—drunk—before?'

'No,' she replied instantly; 'never before yesterday evening.'

'Be frank,' I urged her, smiling sadly.

'Why should I not be frank, madame?' she said, with a grave, gentle appeal.

It was as if she had said: 'We are talking woman to woman. I know one of your secrets. You can guess mine. The male is present, but he is deaf. What reason, therefore, for deceit?'

'I am much obliged to you,' I breathed.

'Not at all,' she said. 'Decidedly he is alcoholic—that sees itself,' she proceeded. 'But drunk—no!... He was always alone.'

'Always alone?'

'Always.'

Her eyes filled. I thought I had never seen a creature more gentle, delicate, yielding, acquiescent, and fair. She was not beautiful, but she had grace and distinction of movement. She was a Parisienne. She had won my sympathy. We met in a moment when my heart needed the companionship of a woman's heart, and I was drawn to her by one of those sudden impulses that sometimes draw women to each other. I cared not what she was. Moreover, she had excited my curiosity. She was a novelty in my life. She was something that I had heard of, and seen—yes, and perhaps envied in secret, but never spoken with. And she shattered all my preconceptions about her.

'You are an old tenant of this house?' I ventured.

'Yes,' she said; 'it suits me. But the great heats are terrible here.'

'You do not leave Paris, then?'

'Never. Except to see my little boy.'

I started, envious of her, and also surprised. It seemed strange that this ribboned and elegant and plastic creature, whose long, thin arms were used only to dalliance, should be a mother.

'So you have a little boy?'

'Yes; he lives with my parents at Meudon. He is four years old.

'Excuse me,' I said. 'Be frank with me once again. Do you love your child, honestly? So many women don't, it appears.'

'Do I love him?' she cried, and her face glowed with her love. 'I adore him!' Her sincerity was touching and overwhelming. 'And he loves me, too. If he is naughty, one has only to tell him that he will make his *petite mère* ill, and he will be good at once. When he is told to obey his grandfather, because his grandfather provides his food, he says bravely: "No, not grandpapa; it is *petite mère*!" Is it not strange he should know that I pay for him? He has a little engraving of the Queen of Italy, and he says it is his *petite mère*. Among the scores of pictures he has he keeps only that one. He takes it to bed with him. It is impossible to deprive him of it.'

She smiled divinely.

'How beautiful!' I said. 'And you go to see him often?'

'As often as I have time. I take him out for walks. I run with him till we reach the woods, where I can have him to myself alone. I never stop; I avoid people. No one except my parents knows that he is my child. One supposes he is a nurse-child, received by my parents. But all the world will know now,' she added, after a pause. 'Last Monday I went to Meudon with my friend Alice, and Alice wanted to buy him some sweets at the grocer's. In the shop I asked him if he would like *dragées*, and he said "Yes." The grocer said to him, "Yes who, young man?" "Yes, *petite mère*," he said, very loudly and bravely. The grocer understood. We all lowered our heads.'

There was something so affecting in the way she half whispered the last phrase, that I could have wept; and yet it was comical, too, and she appreciated that.

'You have no child, madame?' she asked me.

'No,' I said. 'How I envy you!'

'You need not,' she observed, with a touch of hardness. 'I have been so unhappy, that I can never be as unhappy again. Nothing matters now. All I wish is to save enough money to be able to live quietly in a little cottage in the country.'

'With your child,' I put in.

'My child will grow up and leave me. He will become a man, and he will forget his *petite mère*.'

'Do not talk like that,' I protested.

She glanced at me almost savagely. I was astonished at the sudden change in her face.

'Why not?' she inquired coldly. 'Is it not true, then? Do you still believe that there is any difference between one man and another? They are all alike—all, all, all! I know. And it is we who suffer, we others.'

'But surely you have some tender souvenir of your child's father?' I said.

'Do I know who my child's father is?' she demanded. 'My child has thirty-six fathers!'

'You seem very bitter,' I said, 'for your age. You are much younger than I am.'

She smiled and shook her honey-coloured hair, and toyed with the ribbons of her *peignoir*.

'What I say is true,' she said gently. 'But, there, what would you have? We hate them, but we love them. They are beasts! beasts! but we cannot do without them!'

Her eyes rested on Diaz for a moment. He slept without the least sound, the stricken and futile witness of our confidences.

'You will take him away from Paris soon, perhaps?' she asked.

'If I can,' I said.

There was a sound of light footsteps on the stair. They stopped at the door, which I remembered we had not shut. I jumped up and went into the passage. Another girl stood in the doorway, in a *peignoir* the exact counterpart of my first visitor's, but rose-coloured. And this one, too, was languorous and had honey-coloured locks. It was as though the mysterious house was full of such creatures, each with her secret lair.

'Pardon, madame,' said my visitor, following and passing me; and then to the newcomer: 'What is it, Alice?'

'It is Monsieur Duchatel who is arrived.'

'Oh!' with a disdainful gesture. '*Je m'en fiche.* Let him go.'

'But it is the nephew, my dear; not the uncle.'

'Ah, the nephew! I come. *Bon soir, madams, et bonne nuit.*'

The two *peignoirs* fluttered down the stairs together. I returned to my Diaz, and seeing his dressing-gown behind the door of the bedroom, I took it and covered him with it.

IV

His first words were:

'Magda, you look like a ghost. Have you been sitting there like that all the time?'

'No,' I said; 'I lay down.'

'Where?'

'By your side.'

'What time is it?'

'Tea-time. The water is boiling.

'Was I dreadful last night?'

'Dreadful? How?'

'I have a sort of recollection of getting angry and stamping about. I didn't do anything foolish?'

'You took a great deal too much of my sedative,' I answered.

'I feel quite well,' he said; 'but I didn't know I had taken any sedative at all. I'm glad I didn't do anything silly last night.'

I ran away to prepare the tea. The situation was too much for me.

'My poor Diaz!' I said, when we had begun to drink the tea, and he was sitting on the edge of the bed, his eyes full of sleep, his chin rough, and his hair magnificently disarranged, 'you did one thing that was silly last night.'

'Don't tell me I struck you?' he cried.

'Oh no!' and I laughed. 'Can't you guess what I mean?'

'You mean I got vilely drunk.'

I nodded.

'Magda,' he burst out passionately, seeming at this point fully to arouse himself, to resume acutely his consciousness, 'why were you late? You said four o'clock. I thought you had deceived me. I thought I had disgusted you, and that you didn't mean to return. I waited more than an hour and a quarter, and then I went out in despair.'

'But I came just afterwards,' I protested. 'You had only to wait a few more minutes. Surely you could have waited a few more minutes?'

'You said four o'clock,' he repeated obstinately.

'It was barely half-past five when I came,' I said.

'I had meant never to drink again,' he went on.

'You were so kind to me. But then, when you didn't come—'

'You doubted me, Diaz. You ought to have been sure of me.'

'I was wrong.'

'No, no!' I said. 'It was I who was wrong. But I never thought that an hour and a half would make any difference.'

There was a pause.

'Ah, Magda, Magda!'—he suddenly began to weep; it was astounding—'remember that you had deserted me once before. Remember that. If you had not done that, my life might have been different. It *would* have been different.'

'Don't say so,' I pleaded.

'Yes, I must say so. You cannot imagine how solitary my life has been.

Magda, I loved you.'

And I too wept.

His accent was sincerity itself. I saw the young girl hurrying secretly out of the Five Towns Hotel. Could it be true that she had carried away with her, unknowing, the heart of Diaz? Could it be true that her panic flight had ruined a career? The faint possibility that it was true made me sick with vain grief.

'And now I am old and forgotten and disgraced,' he said.

'How old are you, Diaz?'

'Thirty-six,' he answered.

'Why,' I said, 'you have thirty years to live.'

'Yes; and what years?'

'Famous years. Brilliant years.'

He shook his head.

'I am done for—' he murmured, and his head sank.

'Are you so weak, then?' I took his hand. 'Are you so weak? Look at me.'

He obeyed, and his wet eyes met mine. In that precious moment I lived.

'I don't know,' he said.

'You could not have looked at me if you had not been strong, very strong,' I said firmly. 'You told me once that you had a house near Fontainebleau. Have you still got it?'

'I suppose so.'

'Let us go there, and—and—see.'

'But—'

'I should like to go,' I insisted, with a break in my voice.

'My God!' he exclaimed in a whisper, 'my God!'

I was sobbing violently, and my forehead was against the rough stuff of his coat.

V

And one morning, long afterwards, I awoke very early, and the murmuring of the leaves of the forest came through the open window. I had known that I should wake very early, in joyous anticipation of that day. And as I lay he lay beside me, lost in the dreamless, boyish, natural sleep that he never sought in vain. He lay, as always, slightly on his right side, with his face a little towards me—his face that was young again, and from which the bane had passed. It was one of the handsomest, fairest faces in the world, one of the most innocent, and one of the strongest; the face of a man who follows his instincts with the direct simplicity of a savage or a child, and whose instincts are sane and powerful. Seen close, perfectly at rest, as I saw it morning after morning, it was full of a special and mysterious attraction. The fine curves of the nostrils and of the lobe of the ear, the masterful lines of the mouth, the contours of the cheek and chin and temples, the tints of the flesh subtly varying from rose to ivory, the golden crown of hair, the soft moustache. I had learned every detail by heart; my eyes had dwelt on them till they had become my soul's inheritance, till they were mystically mine, drawing me ever towards them, as a treasure draws. Gently moving, I would put my ear close, close, and listen to the breath of life as it entered regularly, almost imperceptibly, vivifying that organism in repose. There is something terrible in the still beauty of sleep. It is as though the spiritual fabric hangs inexplicably over the precipice of death. It seems impossible, or at least miraculous, that the intake and the expulsion upon which existence depends should continue thus, minute by minute, hour by hour. It is as though one stood on the very confines of life, and could one trace but one step more, one single step, one would unveil the eternal secret. I would not listen long; the torture was too sweet, too exquisite, and I would gently slide back to my place.... His hand was on the counterpane, near to my breast—the broad hand of the pianist, with a wrist of incredible force, and the fingers tapering suddenly at the end to a point. I let my own descend on it as softly as snow. Ah, ravishing contact! He did not move. And while my small hand touched his I gazed into the spaces of the bedroom, with its walls of faded blue tapestry and its white curtains, and its marble and rosewood, and they seemed to hold peace, as the hollows of a field hold dew; they seemed to hold happiness as a great tree holds sunlight in its branches; and outside was the murmuring of the leaves of the forest and the virginal freshness of the morning.

Surely he must wake earlier that day! I pursed my lips and blew tenderly, mischievously, on his cheek, lying with my cheek full on the pillow, so that I could watch him. The muscles of his mouth twitched, his inner being appeared to protest. And then began the first instinctive blind movement of the day with him. His arms came forward and found my neck, and drew me forcibly to him, and then, just before our lips touched, he opened his eyes and shut them again. So it occurred every morning. Ere even his brain had resumed activity his heart had felt its need of me. This it was that was so wonderful, so overpowering! And the kiss, languid and yet warm, heavy with a human scent, with the scent of the night, honest, sensuous, and long—long! As I lay thus, clasped in his arms, I half closed my eyes, and looked into his eyes through my lashes, smiling, and all was a delicious blur....

It was the summit of bliss! No! I have never mounted higher! I asked myself, astounded, what I had done that I should receive such happiness, what I had done that existence should have no flaw for me. And what *had* I done? I know not, I know not. It passes me. I am lost in my joy. For I had not even cured him. I had anticipated painful scenes, interminable struggles, perhaps a relapse. But nothing of the kind. He had simply ceased at once the habit—that was all. We never left each other. And his magnificent constitution had perfectly recovered itself in a few months. I had done nothing.

'Magda,' he murmured indistinctly, drawing his mouth an inch away from mine, 'why can't your dark hair always be loose over your shoulders like that? It is glorious!'

'What ideas you have!' I murmured, more softly than he. 'And do you know what it is to-day?'

'No.'

'You've forgotten?' I pouted.

'Yes.'

'Guess.'

'No; you must tell me. Not your birthday? Not mine?'

'It's just a year since I met you,' I whispered timidly.

Our mouths met again, and, so enlocked, we rested, savouring the true savour of life. And presently my hand stole up to his head and stroked his curls.

Every morning he began to practise at eight o'clock, and continued till eleven. The piano, a Steinway in a hundred Steinways, was in the further of the two drawing-rooms. He would go into the room smoking a cigarette, and when he had thrown away the cigarette I would leave him. And as soon as I had closed the door the first notes would resound, slow and solemn, of the five-finger exercises with which he invariably commenced his studies. That morning, as often, I sat writing in the enclosed garden. I always wrote in pencil on my knee. The windows of the drawing-room were wide open, and Diaz' music filled the garden. The sheer beauty of his tone was such that to hear him strike even an isolated note gave pleasure. He created beauty all the time. His five-finger exercises were lovely patterns of sound woven with exact and awful deliberation. It seemed impossible that these should be the same bald and meaningless inventions which I had been wont to repeat. They were transformed. They were music. The material in which he built them was music itself, enchanting the ear as much by the quality of the tone as by the impeccable elegance of the form. To hear Diaz play a scale, to catch that measured, tranquil succession of notes, each a different jewel of equal splendour, each dying precisely when the next was born—this was to perceive at last what music is made of, to have glimpses of the divine magic that is the soul of the divinest art. I used to believe that nothing could surpass the beauty of a scale, until Diaz, after writing formal patterns in the still air innumerably, and hypnotizing me with that sorcery, would pass suddenly to the repetition of fragments of Bach. And then I knew that hitherto he had only been trying to be more purely and severely mechanical than a machine, and that now the interpreter was at work. I have heard him repeat a passage fifty times—and so slowly!—and each rendering seemed more beautiful than the last; and it was more beautiful than the last. He would extract the final drop of beauty from the most beautiful things in the world. Washed, drenched in this circumambient ether of beauty, I wrote my verse. Perhaps it may appear almost a sacrilege that I should have used the practising of a Diaz as a background for my own creative activity. I often thought so. But when one has but gold, one must put it to lowly use. So I wrote, and he passed from Bach to Chopin.

Usually he would come out into the garden for five minutes at half-past nine to smoke a cigarette, but that morning it had struck ten before the music ceased. I saw him. He walked absent-minded along the terrace in the strange silence that had succeeded. He was wearing his riding-breeches, for we habitually rode at eleven. And that morning I did not hide my work when he came. It was, in fact, finished; the time had arrived to disclose it. He stopped in front of me in the sunlight, utterly preoccupied with himself and his labours. He had the rapt look on his face which results from the terrible mental and spiritual strain of practising as he practised.

'Satisfied?' I asked him.

He frowned.

'There are times when one gets rather inspired,' he said, looking at me, as it were, without seeing me. 'It's as if the whole soul gets into one's hands. That's what's wanted.'

'You had it this morning?'

SACRED AND PROFANE LOVE

'A bit.'

He smiled with candid joy.

'While I was listening—' I began.

'Oh!' he broke in impulsively, violently, 'it isn't you that have to listen. It's I that have to listen. It's the player that has to listen. He's got to do more than listen. He's got to be *in* the piano with his inmost heart. If he isn't on the full stretch of analysis the whole blessed time, he might just as well be turning the handle of a barrel-organ.'

He always talked about his work during the little 'recess' which he took in the middle of the morning. He pretended to be talking to me, but it was to himself that he talked. He was impatient if I spoke.

'I shall be greater than ever,' he proceeded, after a moment. And his attitude towards himself was so disengaged, so apart and aloof, so critically appreciative, that it was impossible to accuse him of egoism. He was, perhaps, as amazed at his own transcendent gift as any other person could be, and he was incapable of hiding his sensations. 'Yes,' he repeated; 'I think I shall be greater than ever. You see, a Chopin player is born; you can't make him. With Chopin it's not a question of intellect. It's all tone with Chopin—*tone,* my child, even in the most bravura passages. You've got to get it.'

'Yes,' I agreed.

He gazed over the tree-tops into the blue sky.

'I may be ready in six months,' he said.

'I think you will,' I concurred, with a judicial air. But I honestly deemed him to be more than ready then.

Twelve months previously he had said: 'With six hours' practice a day for two years I shall recover what I have lost.'

He had succeeded beyond his hopes.

'Are you writing in that book?' he inquired carelessly as he threw down the cigarette and turned away.

'I have just finished something,' I replied.

'Oh!' he said, 'I'm glad you aren't idle. It's so boring.'

He returned to the piano, perfectly incurious about what I did, self-absorbed as a god. And I was alone in the garden, with the semicircle of trees behind me, and the façade of the old house and its terrace in front. And lying on the lawn, just under the terrace, was the white end of the cigarette which he had abandoned; it breathed upwards a thin spiral of blue smoke through the morning sunshine, and then it ceased to breathe. And the music recommenced, on a different plane, more brilliantly than before. It was as though, till then, he had been laboriously building the bases of a tremendous triumphal arch, and that now the two wings met, dazzlingly, soaringly, in highest heaven, and the completed arch became a rainbow glittering in the face of the infinite. He played two of his great concert pieces, and their intricate melodies—brocaded, embroidered, festooned—poured themselves through the windows into the garden in a procession majestic and impassioned, perturbing the intent soul of the solitary listener, swathing her in intoxicating sound. It was the unique virtuoso born again, proudly displaying the ultimate sublime end of all those slow-moving exercises to which he had subdued his fingers. Not for ten years had I heard him play so.

When we first came into the house I had said bravely to myself: 'His presence shall not deter me from practising as I have always done.' And one afternoon I had sat down to the piano full of determination to practise without fear of him, without self-consciousness. But before my hands had touched the keys shame took me, unreasoning, terror-struck shame, and I knew in an instant that while he lived I should never more play the piano. He laughed lightly when I told him, and I called myself silly. Yet now, as I sat in the garden, I saw how right I had been. And I wondered that I should ever have had the audacity even to dream of playing in his house; the idea was grotesque. And he did not ask me to play, save when there arrived new orchestral music arranged for four hands. Then I steeled myself to the ordeal of playing with him, because he wished to try over the music. And he would thank me, and say that pianoforte duets were always very enjoyable. But he did not pretend that I was not an amateur, and he never—thank God!—suggested that we should attempt *Tristan* again....

At last he finished. And I heard distantly the bell which he had rung for his glass of milk. And, remembering that I was not ready for the ride, I ran with guilty haste into the house and upstairs.

The two bay horses were waiting, our English groom at their heads, when I came out to the porch. Diaz was impatiently tapping his boot with his whip. He was not in the least a sporting man, but he loved the sensation of riding, and the groom would admit that he rode passably; but he loved more to strut in breeches, and to imitate in little ways the sporting man. I had learnt to ride in order to please him.

'Come along,' he exclaimed.

His eyes said: 'You are always late.' And I was. Some people always know exactly what point they have reached in the maze and jungle of the day, just as mariners are always aware, at the back of their minds, of the state of the tide. But I was not born so.

Diaz helped me to mount, and we departed, jingling through the gate and across the road into a glade of the forest, one of those long sandy defiles, banked on either side, and over-shadowed with tall oaks, which pierce the immense forest like rapiers. The sunshine slanted through the crimsoning leafwork and made irregular golden patches on the dark sand to the furthest limit of the perspective. And though we could not feel the autumn wind, we could hear it in the tree-tops, and it had the sound of the sea. The sense of well-being and of joy was exquisite. The beauty of horses, timid creatures, sensitive and graceful and irrational as young girls, is a thing apart; and what is strange is that their vast strength does not seem incongruous with it. To be above that proud and lovely organism, listening, apprehensive, palpitating, nervous far beyond the human, to feel one's self almost part of it by intimate contact, to yield to it, and make it yield, to draw from it into one's self some of its exultant vitality—in a word, to ride—yes, I could comprehend Diaz' fine enthusiasm for that! I could share it when he was content to let the horses amble with noiseless hoofs over the soft ways. But when he would gallop, and a strong wind sprang up to meet our faces, and the earth shook and thundered, and the trunks of the trees raced past us, then I was afraid. My fancy always saw him senseless at the foot of a tree while his horse calmly cropped the short grass at the sides of the path, or with his precious hand twisted and maimed! And I was in agony till he reined in. I never dared to speak to him of this fear, nor even hint to him that the joy was worth less than the peril. He would have been angry in his heart, and something in him stronger than himself would have forced him to increase the risks. I knew him! ... Ah! but when we went gently, life seemed to be ideal for me, impossibly perfect! It seemed to contain all that I could ever have demanded of it.

I looked at him sideways, so noble and sane and self-controlled. And the days in Paris had receded, far and dim and phantom-like. Was it conceivable that they had once been real, and that we had lived through them? And was this Diaz, the world-renowned darling of capitals, riding by me, a woman whom he had met by fantastic chance? Had he really hidden himself in my arms from the cruel stare of the world and the insufferable curiosity of admirers who, instead of admiring, had begun to pity? Had I in truth saved him? Was it I who would restore him to his glory? Oh, the astounding romance that my life had been! And he was with me! He shared my life, and I his! I wondered what would happen when he returned to his bright kingdom. I was selfish enough to wish that he might never return to his kingdom, and that we might ride and ride for ever in the forest.

And then we came to a circular clearing, with an iron cross in the middle, where roads met, a place such as occurs magically in some ballade of Chopin's. And here we drew rein on the leaf-strewn grass, breathing quickly, with reddened cheeks, and the horses nosed each other, with long stretchings of the neck and rattling of bits.

'So you've been writing again?' said Diaz, smiling quizzically.

'Yes,' I answered. 'I've been writing a long time, but I haven't let *you* know anything about it; and just to-day I've finished it.'

'What is it—another novel?'

'No; a little drama in verse.'

'Going to publish it?'

'Why, naturally.'

Diaz was aware that I enjoyed fame in England and America. He was probably aware that my books had brought me a considerable amount of money. He had read some of my works, and found them excellent— indeed, he was quite proud of my talent. But he did not, he could not, take altogether seriously either my talent or my fame. I knew that he always regarded me as a child gracefully playing at a career. For him there was only one sort of fame; all the other sorts were shadows. A supreme violinist might, perhaps, approach the real thing, in his generous mind; but he was incapable of honestly believing that any fame compared with that of a pianist. The other fames were very well, but they were paste to the precious stone, gewgaws to amuse simple persons. The sums paid to sopranos struck him as merely ridiculous in their enormity. He could not be called conceited; nevertheless, he was magnificently sure that he had been, and still was, the most celebrated person in the civilized world. Certainly he had no superiors in fame, but he would not admit the possibility of equals. Of course, he never argued such a point; it was a tacit assumption, secure from argument. And with that he profoundly reverenced the great composers. The death of Brahms affected him for years. He regarded it as an occasion for universal sorrow. Had Brahms condescended to play the piano, Diaz would have turned the pages for him, and deemed himself honoured—him whom queens had flattered!

'Did you imagine,' I began to tease him, after a pause, 'that while you are working I spend my time in merely existing?'

'You exist—that is enough, my darling,' he said. 'Strange that a beautiful woman can't understand that in existing she is doing her life's work!'

And he leaned over and touched my right wrist below the glove.

'You dear thing!' I murmured, smiling. 'How foolish you can be!'

'What's the drama about?' he asked.

'About La Vallière,' I said.

'La Vallière! But that's the kind of subject I want for my opera!'

'Yes,' I said; 'I have thought so.'

'Could you turn it into a libretto, my child?'

'No, dearest.'

'Why not?'

'Because it already is a libretto. I have written it as such.'

'For me?'

'For whom else?'

And I looked at him fondly, and I think tears came to my eyes.

'You are a genius, Magda!' he exclaimed. 'You leave nothing undone for me. The subject is the very thing to suit Villedo.'

'Who is Villedo?'

'My jewel, you don't know who Villedo is! Villedo is the director of the Opéra Comique in Paris, the most artistic opera-house in Europe. He used to beg me every time we met to write him an opera.'

'And why didn't you?'

'Because I had neither the subject nor the time. One doesn't write operas after lunch in hotel parlours; and as for a good libretto—well, outside Wagner, there's only one opera in the world with a good libretto, and that's *Carmen*.'

Diaz, who had had a youthful operatic work performed at the Royal School of Music in London, and whose numerous light compositions for the pianoforte had, of course, enjoyed a tremendous vogue, was much more serious about his projected opera than I had imagined. He had frequently mentioned it to me, but I had not thought the idea was so close to his heart as I now perceived it to be. I had written the libretto to amuse myself, and perhaps him, and lo! he was going to excite himself; I well knew the symptoms.

'You wrote it in that little book,' he said. 'You haven't got it in your pocket?'

'No,' I answered. 'I haven't even a pocket.'

He would not laugh.

'Come,' he said—'come, let's see it.'

He gathered up his loose rein and galloped off. He could not wait an instant.

'Come along!' he cried imperiously, turning his head.

'I am coming,' I replied; 'but wait for me. Don't leave me like that, Diaz.'

The old fear seized me, but nothing could stop him, and I followed as fast as I dared.

'Where is it?' he asked, when we reached home.

'Upstairs,' I said.

And he came upstairs behind me, pulling my habit playfully, in an effort to persuade us both that his impatience was a simulated one. I had to find my keys and unlock a drawer. I took the small, silk-bound volume from the back part of the drawer and gave it to him.

'There!' I exclaimed. 'But remember lunch is ready.'

He regarded the book.

'What a pretty binding!' he said. 'Who worked it?'

'I did.'

'And, of course, your handwriting is so pretty, too!' he added, glancing at the leaves. '"La Vallière, an opera in three acts."'

We exchanged a look, each of us deliciously perturbed, and then he ran off with the book.

He had to be called three times from the garden to lunch, and he brought the book with him, and read it in snatches during the meal, and while sipping his coffee. I watched him furtively as he turned over the pages.

'Oh, you've done it!' he said at length—'you've done it! You evidently have a gift for libretto. It is neither more nor less than perfect! And the subject is wonderful!'

He rose, walked round the table, and, taking my head between his hands, kissed me.

'Magda,' he said, 'you're the cleverest girl that was ever born.'

'Then, do you think you will compose it?' I asked, joyous.

'Do I think I will compose it! Why, what do you imagine? I've already begun. It composes itself. I'm now going to read it all again in the garden. Just see that I'm not worried, will you?'

'You mean you don't want me there. You don't care for me any more.'

It amused me to pretend to pout.

'Yes,' he laughed; 'that's it. I don't care for you any more.'

He departed.

'Have no fear!' I cried after him. 'I shan't come into your horrid garden!'

His habit was to resume his practice at three o'clock. The hour was then half-past one. I wondered whether he would allow himself to be seduced from the piano that afternoon by the desire to compose. I hoped not, for there could be no question as to the relative importance to him of the two activities. To my surprise, I heard the piano at two o'clock, instead of at three, and it continued without intermission till five. Then he came, like a sudden wind, on to the terrace where I was having tea. Diaz would never take afternoon tea. He seized my hand impulsively.

'Come down,' he said—'down under the trees there.'

'What for?'

'I want you.'

'But, Diaz, let me put my cup down. I shall spill the tea on my dress.'

'I'll take your cup.'

'And I haven't nearly finished my tea, either. And you're hurting me.'

'I'll bring you a fresh cup,' he said. 'Come, come!'

And he dragged me off, laughing, to the lower part of the garden, where were two chairs in the shade. And I allowed myself to be dragged.

'There! Sit down. Don't move. I'll fetch your tea.'

And presently he returned with the cup.

'Now that you've nearly killed me,' I said, 'and spoilt my dress, perhaps you'll explain.'

He produced the silk-bound book of manuscript from his pocket and put it in my unoccupied hand.

'I want you to read it to me aloud, all of it,' he said.

'Really?'

'Really.'

'What a strange boy you are!' I chided.

Then I drank the tea, straightened my features into seriousness, and began to read.

The reading occupied less than an hour. He made no remark when it was done, but held out his hand for the book, and went out for a walk. At dinner he was silent till the servants had gone. Then he said musingly:

'That scene in the cloisters between Louise and De Montespan is a great idea. It will be magnificent; it will be the finest thing in the opera. What a subject you have found! what a subject!' His tone altered. 'Magda, will you do something to oblige me?'

'If it isn't foolish.'

'I want you to go to bed.'

'Out of the way?' I smiled.

'Go to bed and to sleep,' he repeated.

'But why?'

'I want to walk about this floor. I must be alone.'

'Well,' I said, 'just to prove how humble and obedient I am, I will go.'

And I held up my mouth to be kissed.

Wondrous, the joy I found in playing the decorative, acquiescent, self-effacing woman to him, the pretty, pouting plaything! I liked him to dismiss me, as the soldier dismisses his charmer at the sound of the bugle. I liked to think upon his obvious conviction that the libretto was less than nothing compared to the music. I liked him to regard the whole artistic productivity of my life as the engaging foible of a pretty woman. I liked him to forget that I had brought him alive out of Paris. I liked him to forget to mention marriage to me. In a word, he was Diaz, and I was his.

And as I lay in bed I even tried to go to sleep, in my obedience, because I knew he would wish it. But I could not easily sleep for anticipating his triumph of the early future. His habits of composition were extremely rapid. It might well occur that he would write the entire opera in a few months, without at all sacrificing the piano. And naturally any operatic manager would be loath to refuse an opera signed by Diaz. Villedo, apparently so famous, would be sure to accept it, and probably would produce it at once. And Diaz would have a double triumph, a dazzling and gorgeous re-entry into the world. He might give his first recital in the same week as the *première* of the opera. And thus his shame would never be really known to the artistic multitude. The legend of a nervous collapse could be insisted on, and the opera itself would form a sufficient excuse for his retirement.... And I should be the secret cause of all this glory—I alone! And no one would ever guess what Diaz owed to me. Diaz himself would never appreciate it. I alone, withdrawn from the common gaze, like a woman of the East, Diaz' secret fountain of strength and balm—I alone should be aware of what I had done. And my knowledge would be enough for me.

I imagine I must have been dreaming when I felt a hand on my cheek.

'Magda, you aren't asleep, are you?'

Diaz was standing over me.

'No, no!' I answered, in a voice made feeble by sleep. And I looked up at him.

'Put something on and come downstairs, will you?'

'What time is it?'

'Oh, I don't know. One o'clock.'

'You've been working for over three hours, then!'

I sat up.

'Yes,' he said proudly. 'Come along. I want to play you my notion of the overture. It's only in the rough, but it's there.'

'You've begun with the overture?'

'Why not, my child? Here's your dressing-gown. Which is the top end of it?'

I followed him downstairs, and sat close by him at the piano, with one limp hand on his shoulder. There was no light in the drawing-rooms, save one candle on the piano. My slipper escaped off my bare foot. As Diaz played he looked at me constantly, demanding my approval, my enthusiasm, which I gave him from a full heart. I thought the music charming, and, of course, as he played it...!

'I shall only have three motives,' he said. 'That's the La Vallière motive. Do you see the idea?'

'You mean she limps?'

'Precisely. Isn't it delightful?'

'She won't have to limp much, you know. She didn't.'

'Just the faintest suggestion. It will be delicious. I can see Morenita in the part. Well, what do you think of it?'

I could not speak. His appeal, suddenly wistful, moved me so. I leaned forward and kissed him.

'Dear girl!' he murmured.

Then he blew out the candle. He was beside himself with excitement.

'Diaz,' I cried, 'what's the matter with you? Do have a little sense. And you've made me lose my slipper.'

'I'll carry you upstairs,' he replied gaily.

A faint illumination came from the hall, so that we could just see each other. He lifted me off the chair.

'No!' I protested, laughing. 'And my slipper.... The servants!'

'Stuff!'

I was a trifle in those arms.

VI

The triumphal re-entry into the world has just begun, and exactly as Diaz foretold. And the life of the forest is over. We have come to Paris, and he has taken Paris, and already he is leaving it for other shores, and I am to follow. At this moment, while I write because I have not slept and cannot sleep, his train rolls out of St. Lazare.

Last night! How glorious! But he is no longer wholly mine. The world has turned his face a little from my face....

It was as if I had never before realized the dazzling significance of the fame of Diaz. I had only once seen him in public. And though he conquered in the Jubilee Hall of the Five Towns, his victory, personal and artistic, at the Opera Comique, before an audience as exacting, haughty, and experienced as any in Europe, was, of course, infinitely more striking—a victory worthy of a Diaz.

I sat alone and hidden at the back of a *baignoire* in the auditorium. I had drawn up the golden grille, by which the occupants of a *baignoire* may screen themselves from the curiosity of the *parterre*. I felt like some caged Eastern odalisque, and I liked so to feel. I liked to exist solely for him, to be mysterious, and to baffle the general gaze in order to be more precious to him. Ah, how I had changed! How he had changed me!

It was Thursday, a subscription night, and, in addition, all Paris was in the theatre, a crowded company of celebrities, of experts, and of perfectly-dressed women. And no one knew who I was, nor why I was there. The vogue of a musician may be universal, but the vogue of an English writer is nothing beyond England and America. I had not been to a rehearsal. I had not met Villedo, nor even the translator of my verse. I had wished to remain in the background, and Diaz had not crossed me. Thus I gazed through the bars of my little cell across the rows of bald heads, and wonderful coiffures, and the waving arms of the conductor, and the restless, gliding bows of the violinists, and saw a scene which was absolutely strange and new to me. And it seemed amazing that these figures which I saw moving and chanting with such grace in a palace garden, authentic to the last detail of historical accuracy, were my La Vallière and my Louis, and that this rich and coloured music which I heard was the same that Diaz had sketched for me on the piano, from illegible scraps of ruled paper, on the edge of the forest. The full miracle of operatic art was revealed to me for the first time.

And when the curtain fell on the opening act, the intoxicating human quality of an operatic success was equally revealed to me for the first time. How cold and distant the success of a novelist compared to this! The auditorium was suddenly bathed in bright light, and every listening face awoke to life as from an enchantment, and flushed and smiled, and the delicatest hands in France clapped to swell the mighty uproar that filled the theatre with praise. Paris, upstanding on its feet, and leaning over balconies and cheering, was charmed and delighted by the fable and the music, in which it found nothing but the sober and pretty elegance that it loves. And Paris applauded feverishly, and yet with a full sense of the value of its applause—given there in the only French theatre where the claque has been suppressed. And then the curtain rose, and La Vallière and Louis tripped mincingly forward to prove that after all they were Morenita and Montfériot, the darlings of their dear Paris, and utterly content with their exclusively Parisian reputation. Three times they came forward. And then the applause ceased, for Paris is not Naples, and it is not Madrid, and the red curtain definitely hid the stage, and the theatre hummed with animated chatter as elegant as Diaz' music, and my ear, that loves the chaste vivacity of the French tongue, was caressed on every side by its cadences.

'This is the very heart of civilization,' I said to myself. 'And even in the forest I could not breathe more freely.'

I stared up absently at Benjamin Constant's blue ceiling, meretricious and still adorable, expressive of the delicious decadence of Paris, and my eyes moistened because the world is so beautiful in such various ways.

Then the door of the *baignoire* opened. It was Diaz himself who appeared. He had not forgotten me in the excitements of the stage and the dressing-rooms. He put his hand lightly on my shoulder, and I glanced at him.

'Well?' he murmured, and gave me a box of bonbons elaborately tied with rich ribbons.

And I murmured, 'Well?'

The glory of his triumph was upon him. But he understood why my eyes were wet, and his fingers moved soothingly on my shoulder.

'You won't come round?' he asked. 'Both Villedo and Morenita are dying to meet you.'

I shook my head, smiling.

'You're satisfied?'

'More than satisfied,' I answered. 'The thing is wonderful.'

'I think it's rather charming,' he said. 'By the way, I've just had an offer from New York for it, and another from Rome.'

I nodded my appreciation.

'You don't want anything?'

'Nothing, thanks,' I said, opening the box of bonbons, 'except these.

Thanks so much for thinking of them.'

'Well—'

And he left me again.

In the second act the legend—has not the tale of La Vallière acquired almost the quality of a legend?—grew in persuasiveness and in magnificence. It was the hour of La Vallière's unwilling ascendancy, and it foreboded also her fall. The situations seemed to me to be poignantly beautiful, especially that in which La Vallière and Montespan and the Queen found themselves together. And Morenita had perceived my meaning with such a sure intuition. I might say that she showed me what I had meant. Diaz, too, had given to my verse a voice than which it appeared impossible that anything could be more appropriate. The whole effect was astonishing, ravishing. And within me—far, far within the recesses of my glowing heart—a thin, clear whisper spoke and said that I, and I alone, was the cause of that beauty of sight and sound. Not Morenita, and not Montfériot, not Diaz himself, but Magda, the self-constituted odalisque, was its author. I had thought of it; I had schemed it; I had fashioned it; I had evoked the emotion in it. The others had but exquisitely embroidered my theme. Without me they must have been dumb and futile. On my shoulders lay the burden and the glory. And though I was amazed, perhaps naively, to see what I had done, nevertheless I had done it—I! The entire opera-house, that complicated and various machine, was simply a means to express me. And it was to my touch on their heartstrings that the audience vibrated. With all my humility, how proud I was—coldly and arrogantly proud, as only the artist can be! I wore my humility as I wore my black gown. Even Diaz could not penetrate to the inviolable place in my heart, where the indestructible egoism defied the efforts of love to silence it. And yet people say there is nothing stronger than love.

At the close of the act, while the ringing applause, much more enthusiastic than before, gave certainty of a genuine and extraordinary success, I could not help blushing. It was as if I was in danger of being discovered as the primal author of all that fleeting loveliness, as if my secret was bound to get about, and I to be forced from my seclusion in order to receive the acclamations of Paris. I played nervously and self-consciously with my fan, and I wrapped my humility closer round me, until at length the tumult died away, and the hum of charming, eager chatter reassured my ears again.

Diaz did not come. The entr'acte stretched out long, and the chatter lost some of its eagerness, and he did not come. Perhaps he could not come. Perhaps he was too much engaged, too much preoccupied, to think of the gallantry which he owed to his mistress. A man cannot always be dreaming of his mistress. A mistress must be reconciled to occasional neglect; she must console herself with chocolates. And they were chocolates from Marquis's, in the Passage des Panoramas....

Then he came, accompanied.

A whirl of high-seasoned, laughing personalities invaded my privacy.

Diaz, smiling humorously, was followed by a man and a cloaked woman.

'Dear lady,' he said, with an intimate formality, 'I present Mademoiselle

Morenita and Monsieur Villedo. They insisted on seeing you. Mademoiselle,

Monsieur—Mademoiselle Peel.'

I stood up.

'All our excuses,' said Villedo, in a low, discreet voice, as he carefully shut the door. 'All our excuses, madame. But it was necessary that I should pay my respects—it was stronger than I.'

And he came forward, took my hand, and raised it to his lips. He is a little finicking man, with a little gray beard, and the red rosette in his button-hole, and a most consummate ease of manner.

'Monsieur,' I replied, 'you are too amiable. And you, madame. I cannot sufficiently thank you both.'

Morenita rushed at me with a swift, surprising movement, her cloak dropping from her shoulders, and taking both my hands, she kissed me impulsively.

'You have genius,' she said; 'and I am proud. I am ashamed that I cannot read English; but I have the intention to learn in order to read your books. Our Diaz says wonderful things of them.'

She is a tall, splendidly-made, opulent creature, of my own age, born for the footlights, with an extremely sweet and thrilling voice, and that slight coarseness or exaggeration of gesture and beauty which is the penalty of the stage. She did not in the least resemble a La Vallière as she stood there gazing at me, with her gleaming, pencilled eyes and heavy, scarlet lips. It seemed impossible that she could refine herself to a La Vallière. But that woman is the drama itself. She would act no matter what. She has always the qualities necessary to a rôle. And the gods have given her green eyes, so that she may be La Vallière to the very life.

I began to thank her for her superb performance.

'It is I who should thank you,' she answered. 'It will be my greatest part. Never have I had so many glorious situations in a part. Do you like my limp?'

She smiled, her head on one side. Success glittered in those orbs.

'You limp adorably,' I said.

'It is my profession to make compliments,' Villedo broke in; and then, turning to Morenita, '*N'est-ce pas, ma belle créature?* But really'—he turned to me again—'but very sincerely, all that there is of most sincerely, dear madame, your libretto is made with a virtuosity astonishing. It is *du théâtre*. And with that a charm, an emotion...! One would say—'

And so it continued, the flattering stream, while Diaz listened, touched, and full of pride.

'Ah!' I said. 'It is not I who deserve praise.'

An electric bell trembled in the theatre.

Morenita picked up her cloak.

'*Mon ami*,' she warned Villedo. 'I must go. Diaz, *mon petit*! you will persuade Mademoiselle Peel to come to the room of the Directeur later. Madame, a few of us will meet there—is it not so, Villedo? We shall count on you, madame. You have hidden yourself too long.'

I glanced at Diaz, and he nodded. As a fact, I wished to refuse; but I could not withstand the seduction of Morenita. She had a physical influence which was unique in my experience.

'I accept,' I said.

'*A tout à l'heure*, then,' she twittered gaily; and they left as they had come, Villedo affectionately toying with Morenita's hand.

Diaz remained behind a moment.

'I am so glad you didn't decline,' he said. 'You see, here in this theatre Morenita is a queen. I wager she has never before in all her life put herself out of the way as she has done for you to-night.'

'Really!' I faltered.

And, indeed, as I pondered over it, the politeness of these people appeared to be marvellous, and so perfectly accomplished. Villedo, who has made a European reputation and rejuvenated his theatre in a dozen years, is doubtless, as he said, a professional maker of compliments. In his position a man must be. But, nevertheless, last night's triumph is officially and very genuinely Villedo's. While as for Morenita and Diaz, the mere idea of these golden stars waiting on me, the librettist, effacing themselves, rendering themselves subordinate at such a moment, was fantastic. It passed the credible.... A Diaz standing silent and deferential, while an idolized prima donna stepped down from her throne to flatter me in her own temple! All that I had previously achieved of renown seemed provincial, insular.

But Diaz took his own right place in the spacious salon of Villedo afterwards, after all the applause had ceased, and the success had been consecrated, and the enraptured audience had gone, and the lights were extinguished in the silent auditorium. It is a room that seems to be furnished with nothing but a grand piano and a large, flat writing-table and a few chairs. On the walls are numberless signed portraits of singers and composers, and antique playbills of the Opéra Comique, together with strange sinister souvenirs of the great fires which have destroyed the house and its patrons in the past. When Diaz led me in, only Villedo and the principal artists and Pouvillon, the conductor, were present. Pouvillon, astonishingly fat, was sitting on the table, idly swinging the electric pendant over his head; while Morenita occupied Villedo's armchair, and Villedo talked to Montfériot and another man in a corner. But a crowd of officials of the theatre ventured on Diaz' heels. And then came Monticelli, the *première danseuse*, in a coat and skirt, and then some of her rivals. And as the terrible Director did not protest, the room continued to fill until it was full to the doors, where stood a semicircle of soiled, ragged scene-shifters and a few fat old women, who were probably dressers. Who could protest on such a night? The democracy of a concerted triumph reigned. Everybody was joyous, madly happy. Everybody had done something; everybody shared the prestige, and the rank and file might safely take generals by the hand.

Diaz was then the centre of attraction. It was recognised that he had entered that sphere from a wider one, bringing with him a radiance brighter than he found there. He was divine last night. All felt that he was divine. He spoke to everyone with an admirable modesty, gaily, his eyes laughing. Several women kissed him, including Morenita. Not that I minded. In the theatre the code is different, coarser, more banal. He alone raised this crowd above its usual level and gave it distinction.

Someone suggested that, as the piano was there, he should play, and the demand ran from mouth to mouth. Villedo, appreciating its audacity, made a gesture to indicate that such a thing could not be asked. But Diaz instantly said that, if it would give pleasure, he would play with pleasure.

And he sat down to the piano, and looked round, smiling, and the room was hushed in a moment, and each face was turned towards him.

'What?' he ejaculated. And then, as no definite recommendation was offered, he said: 'Do you wish that I improvise?'

The idea was accepted with passionate, noisy enthusiasm.

A cold perspiration broke out over my whole body. I must have turned very pale.

'You are not ill, madame?' asked that ridiculous fop, Montfèriot, who had been presented to me, and was whispering the most fatuous compliments.

'No, I thank you.'

The fact was that Diaz, since his retirement, had not yet played to anyone except myself. This was his first appearance. I was afraid for him. I trembled for him. I need not have done. He was absolutely master of his powers. His fingers announced, quite simply, one of the most successful airs from *La Vallière*, and then he began to decorate it with an amazing lacework of variations, and finished with a bravura display such as no pianist could have surpassed. The performance, marvellous in itself, was precisely suited to that audience, and it electrified the audience; it electrified even me. Diaz fought his way through kisses and embraces to Villedo, who stood on his toes and wept and put his arms round Diaz' neck.

'*Cher maître*,' he cried, 'you overwhelm us!'

'You are too kind, all of you,' said Diaz. 'I must ask permission to retire. I have to conduct Mademoiselle Peel to her hotel, and there is much for me to do during the night. You know I start very early to-morrow.'

'*Hélas!*' Morenita sighed.

I had blushed. Decidedly I behaved like a girl last night. But, indeed, the new, swift realization, as Diaz singled me out of that multitude, that after all he utterly belonged to me, that he was mine alone, was more than I could bear with equanimity. I was the proudest woman in the universe. I scorned the lot of all other women.

The adieux were exchanged, and there were more kisses. '*Au revoir! Bon voyage*! Much success over there.'

The majority of these good, generous souls were in tears.

Villedo opened a side-door, and we escaped into a corridor, only Morenita and one or two others accompanying us to the street.

And on the pavement a carpet had been laid. The electric brougham was waiting. I gathered up my skirt and sprang in. Diaz followed, smiling at me. He put his head out of the window and said a few words. Morenita blew a kiss. Villedo bowed profoundly. The carriage moved in the direction of the boulevard.... I had carried him off. Oh, the exquisite dark intimacy of the interior of that smooth-rolling brougham! When, after the theatre, a woman precedes a man into a carriage, does she not publish and glory in the fact that she is his? Is it not the most delicious of avowals? There is something in the enforced bend of one's head as one steps in. And when the man shuts the door with a masculine snap—

I wondered idly what Morenita and Villedo thought of our relations. They must surely guess.

We went down the boulevard and by the Rue Royale into the Place de la Concorde, where vehicles flitted mysteriously in a maze of lights under the vast dome of mysterious blue. And Paris, in her incomparable toilette of a June night, seemed more than ever the passionate city of love that she is, recognising candidly, with the fearless intellectuality of the Latin temperament, that one thing only makes life worth living. How soft was the air! How languorous the pose of the dim figures that passed us half hidden in other carriages! And in my heart was the lofty joy of work done, definitely accomplished, and a vista of years of future pleasure. My happiness was ardent and yet calm—a happiness beyond my hopes, beyond what a mortal has the right to dream of. Nothing could impair it, not even Diaz' continued silence as to a marriage between us, not even the imminent brief separation that I was to endure.

'My child,' said Diaz suddenly, 'I'm very hungry. I've never been so hungry.'

'You surely didn't forget to have your dinner?' I exclaimed.

'Yes, I did,' he admitted like a child; 'I've just remembered.'

'Diaz!' I pouted, and for some strange reason my bliss was intensified, 'you are really terrible! What can I do with you? You will eat before you leave me. I must see to that. We can get something for you at the hotel, perhaps.'

'Suppose we go to a supper restaurant?' he said.

Without waiting for my reply, he seized the dangling end of the speaking-tube and spoke to the driver, and we swerved round and regained the boulevard.

And in the private room of a great, glittering restaurant, one of a long row of private rooms off a corridor, I ate strawberries and cream and sipped champagne while Diaz went through the entire menu of a supper.

'Your eyes look sad,' he murmured, with a cigar between his teeth. 'What is it? We shall see each other again in a fortnight.'

He was to resume his career by a series of concerts in the United States. A New York agent, with the characteristic enterprise of New York agents, had tracked Diaz even into the forest and offered him two hundred and fifty thousand dollars for forty concerts on the condition that he played at no concert before he played in New York. And in order to reach New

York in time for the first concert, it was imperative that he should catch the *Touraine* at Havre. I was to follow in a few days by a Hamburg-American liner. Diaz had judged it more politic that we should not travel together. In this he was undoubtedly right.

I smiled proudly.

'I am both sad and happy,' I answered.

He moved his chair until it touched mine, and put his arm round my neck, and brought my face close to his.

'Look at me,' he said.

And I looked into his large, splendid eyes.

'You mustn't think,' he whispered, 'that, because I don't talk about it,

I don't feel that I owe everything to you.'

I let my face fall on his breast. I knew I had flushed to the ears.

'My poor boy,' I sobbed, 'if you talk about that I shall never forgive you.'

It was heaven itself. No woman has ever been more ecstatically happy than

I was then.

He rang for the bill.

We parted at the door of my hotel. In the carriage we had exchanged one long, long kiss. At the last moment I wanted to alter the programme, go with him to his hotel to assist in his final arrangements, and then see him off at early morning at the station. But he refused. He said he could not bear to part from me in public. Perhaps it was best so. Just as I turned away he put a packet into my hand. It contained seven banknotes for ten thousand francs each, money that it had been my delight to lend him from time to time. Foolish, vain, scrupulous boy! I knew not where he had obtained

Printed in the USA
CPSIA information can be obtained
at www.ICGtesting.com
LVHW010725130124
768850LV00003B/217